"Friends go missing, lovers are separated, yet Carla Guelfenbein, a writer with a fierce and tender imagination, makes this novel all about presence: the insistent presence of the past, the presence of possibility and hope. Every point of absence generates probing thought and fervent emotions. Guelfenbein has filled her canvas with mesmerizing, intricate life, leaving no blank spaces."

—Joanna Scott, author of *The Manikin*

"In this kaleidoscopic novel of loves, longings, and disappearances, Carla Guelfenbein brilliantly enfolds mysteries that distances of time and space strive to conceal. It's a bonus that her writing sparkles. I know of no other non-native writer since Federico García Lorca who has seen Manhattan with such original precision."

—Todd Gitlin, author of *The Sixties*

"A mesmerizing novel that explores women's quest for identity as well as independence. Using the character of Gabriela Mistral and her companion Doris Dana as the centerpiece, these stories are intertwined with grace and passion. An extraordinary book and a delight to read for its inquisitive nature and audacious perspective."

—Marjorie Agosín, recipient of the Gabriela Mistral Medal of Honor for Lifetime Achievement

one

in me

i never

loved

CARLA GUELFENBEIN

*Translated from the Spanish
by Neil Davidson*

other press

NEW YORK

Copyright © 2019 Carla Guelfenbein
Originally published in Spanish as *La estación de las mujeres* in 2019
by Penguin Random House Grupo Editorial, S.A., Santiago, Chile.
English translation copyright © 2021 Other Press

Production editor: Yvonne E. Cárdenas
Text designer: Jennifer Daddio / Bookmark Design & Media Inc.
This book was set in Horley OS Light and Dear Sarah
by Alpha Design & Composition of Pittsfield, NH.

1 3 5 7 9 10 8 6 4 2

Library of Congress Cataloging-in-Publication Data
Names: Guelfenbein, Carla, 1959- author. | Davidson, Neil, 1966- translator.
Title: One in me I never loved / Carla Guelfenbein ; translated from the
Spanish by Neil Davidson.
Other titles: Estación de las mujeres. English
Description: New York : Other Press, [2021]
Identifiers: LCCN 2021005449 (print) | LCCN 2021005450 (ebook) |
ISBN 9781590518724 (paperback) | ISBN 9781590518731 (ebook)
Classification: LCC PQ8098.417.U35 E8813 2021 (print) |
LCC PQ8098.417.U35 (ebook) | DDC 863/.7—dc23
LC record available at https://lccn.loc.gov/2021005449
LC ebook record available at https://lccn.loc.gov/2021005450

FOR

my grandmothers,

my mother,

AND

my daughter

One in me I killed:

I never loved her.

She blazed like the mountain

cactus flower.

—GABRIELA MISTRAL, *"The Other"*

margarita

the last time Jorge wanted to have sex with me, I asked him to use a condom. One with a Jenny Holzer slogan on it. That was three weeks ago, before the vacation ended and his students got back from their yachts and other summer retreats. He stared and then burst out laughing. He didn't ask who Jenny Holzer was. "I mean it," I said. "If you want to make love, it'll have to be with a condom. And kindly make it a Jenny Holzer condom." We were lying on the bed, him naked, me with my nightshirt around my ankles. Children's shouts carried in from outside. Maybe they were playing soccer in the streets deserted by the students. Jorge stood up and regarded me from the heights of his nudity. He looked utterly confident—imagining, I suppose, that his virility would quell my insurrection. I noticed that the flesh on his stomach had gone. From some part of his life he extracts time to go to the gym. From the part that should be for me, clearly, because I see less and less of him. I turned over and pulled the sheet right up over my head. My body, unlike his, is expanding and collapsing a little more each day, creasing, wilting, falling in on itself in weary rolls. Sometimes I hardly recognize it as mine.

Someone else's body is a place for your mind to go

Today is my fifty-sixth birthday. It's nine in the morning and I'm sitting on a bench carved with Jenny Holzer texts. Phrases of hers have gone onto T-shirts, golf balls, caps, mugs, and even condoms. The bench is in the public garden opposite the gates of Barnard College, where dozens of shameless butterflies flit in and out, with skirts up to their crotch and backpacks on their shoulders. I watch them. I watch and wait for Jorge to appear with one of them hanging from his arm. Brakes squeal. A siren drills the air. I watch the concentric movements of the day go by.

Murder has its sexual side

I'd hoped that Jorge might wish me happy birthday this morning, that he might give me a box of chocolates, a flower, or a soothing word to fortify me against the ravages of time, and, why not, I also cherished the hope of a surprise screw. But there was none of that. He woke up, went to the bathroom, doubtless masturbated to porn on his cell phone, got dressed, picked up the leather briefcase every academic in the world carries, gave me a peck on the forehead, and left. That's why I'm here. Sitting on Jenny's bench while I wait for something to happen, for something to blow apart and end this drift into a future that long since ceased to be unpredictable. Yes, yes, what I want, what I'm really waiting for, is for my husband to waltz through that gate with a girl on his arm and for everything to go to hell.

Jorge, Jorge," I shook my husband one night as he snored next to me with a pillow over his head.

"Eh?"

"I have a premonition that something very bad is going to happen."

"Uhhhhhh."

"Really, really bad. I mean it."

"Do you want me to go and look?" came from the depths of the pillow, in that sullen drone that lodged in his throat all too many years ago.

"Where do you plan on looking?" Did he happen to know of a place where you could go and scrutinize future events?

"I don't know, wherever you say."

I was left pondering. The idea that there could be a kind of showcase somewhere containing all possible future events was intriguing. Because in the end, if you think about it, an event that actually happens is just the one somebody picked out from the thousands of possibles awaiting their turn in the display.

"Macy's. Yes, Macy's," I repeated more firmly.

My husband opened his eyes in the dark. Two black marbles stared at me in disbelief. He lay like that for a couple of seconds, unmoving, bewildered but alert, then fell asleep again.

But his eyes were still open.

To test how much of his awareness remained intact, I said: "Yesterday Analía told me she'd seen you screwing that Italian woman in the professors' bathroom."

Analía is the Mexican woman who cleans the professors' offices. The Italian woman is a distinguished academic who arrived a few months back to join the exclusive men's club of the Columbia University Physics Department. When Jorge didn't answer and his stare didn't alter, I took it that he really was asleep. It was a unique opportunity to look him in the eye and say whatever I pleased. I started by telling him how much I loved him.

"Hey, do you know I'm crazy about you and that you drive me wild sometimes? I imagine things. Things like you licking me down there and then kissing me so I taste my smell in your mouth. Or straddling me, holding me down and sticking it in my mouth. Why have you never done anything like that with me? Isn't it what you do with your butterflies?"

Suddenly my fantasies evaporated, to be replaced by a feeling of combative freedom.

Use what is dominant in a culture to change it quickly

His eyes were still open. I shook him lightly to check if he was still asleep.

"Shall I tell you something, Jorge, Jorgito?

"Do you know you're often quite disarmingly ridiculous? Like when you talk about Nicanor Parra as though he'd been your best friend, though you only met him once, just the once, and exchanged a few words at most! Or when you go up to a girl who could be your daughter and talk to her in her jargon as if you were a member of her tribe, or when you listen to someone but don't actually listen, just bide your time till you can cut in and start on the one subject you really care about: yourself. Or when you arrive somewhere quite certain that everyone is going to turn around and do homage to the famous professor DíazLefert (you made sure from the start that the two surnames would be pronounced as one, so that that Díaz, so commonplace in our class-ridden country, would be joined forever to the foreign surname you got from some ancestor too remote for you to have inherited any of his European traits), but no one actually notices you're there. Or when a Renaissance mood takes you, or you have a personal renaissance, shall we say, and buy canary-yellow pants two sizes too small that don't stretch over your nonexistent buttocks. Because, yes, Jorgito, believe it or not, men's asses shrivel too, and what's left under their pants are a couple of bones no one much wants to pinch. Did you know that?"

I stopped. I took a breath. A tingle ran down my spine. I realized I was shaking.

"Jorge DíazLefert," I whispered. "I . . ."

a girl in giant headphones comes up to my bench opposite Barnard College and asks the way to the auditorium. I stand up and whisper directions, forcing her to take off the contraptions, which make a noise like glass being crushed as they hang around her neck. Before I go back to my place on the bench I look at the phrase I've been sitting on.

Push yourself to the limit as often as possible

i sit down again. Aware this time that I'm covering up Holzer's telling phrase. Here's hoping that no other living being gets the same idea, decides to push themselves to the limit so that they and I end up colliding at our limits in the beyond, destroying each other mercilessly as two beings tend to do when they reach for the same star. But what are the chances of a former primary school teacher, dragged out to New York by her husband (whom she is so suspicious of that she sits for hours opposite the gates of the university where he works to catch him out, and who spends the rest of her days pointlessly ruminating)—what are the chances of her pushing herself to the limit?

I think of all the women who wait unmoving in the shadows. Waiting is a way of disappearing, especially when what you are waiting for, with a mixture of masochism and perversion, is for your husband to appear with a girl clinging to his arm.

doris

it is half past eleven one morning in this year of 1948. Light though the unopened letter is, Doris Dana can almost see it sinking into the counterpane of her unmade bed. Her head rings with the fish seller's unending whistling and the clatter of his cart on the cobbles. And with the knife grinder's howls: Briiiiing out your kniiiiiiiiives and scissooooors! She knows him. His name is Sid, and he boasts of being the finest knife grinder in New York. She covers her ears with her hands and then presses her fingertips to her tired forehead. It is the third letter from Gabriela in five days. Or the fourth? She does not need to open it to know the words are bitter. She lies back on the pillow. Her head hurts. The pain is unremitting, and so is the need to lose herself, to fill the room with something other than Gabriela's voice. She can hear her in her temples, a giant, thudding heartbeat that fills everything, leaving her spiritless and with a feeling of nowhereness, emptiness, littleness. But she can't tell her that. It could mean the end. Although she knows too that for Gabriela there is no end. She knows she can do or say what she likes, and Gabriela will still cling to that "us" like an old squirrel clutching the last hazelnut in the park. *Who's with you? Did you sleep well? Do you ever think of this poor old fellow? Because he thinks about you all the time. Where are you now, what are you doing, what are you thinking, what is the expression in your eyes, on your mouth?*

She remembers Aline's last kiss the night before. They met again in the Steeples' salon after fifteen years. She can't remember how she came to be there, but she does have a clear image of the chandelier glinting on the gentlemen's bald heads and their wives' powdered faces. She also remembers Aline standing haughtily on the majestic staircase, one foot a step above the other, a gloved hand holding up a cigarette and the other steadying her on the bannister. She knew that expression of hers well, eyes narrowed as though she were peering between lace curtains. Her shortsightedness had earned her jibes as a girl but with the years had lent her an air of mystery and indifference. She remembered Aline's younger sister, Elizabeth, found lifeless in a men's residence near Columbia University two years before. The family paid the press a lot of money to cover up the tragedy. Only a few people learned the truth. Perhaps that was why she approached Aline last night after so long. Few things attracted her so much as the proximity of death.

As girls they had played together at the Moss Lots mansion, in the playhouse Doris's father had built for her and her sisters in a corner of the grounds. Aline was too small-boned and disjointed then. Doris and her sisters used to stuff wads of wet paper in her mouth, and not stop until tears ran down her reddened cheeks. Aline had been at Moss Lots that evening more than twenty years earlier, when they had gone into the living room and found the Dana girls' father sitting in front of the fireplace with a Colt M1911 pressed to his temple. Their mother was squatting in front of him with her hands on his knees. They were both drunk. Without taking the gun from his head, their father moved the barrel back and forth so that it seemed to mark time like a clock pendulum. The girls sat very close together on the floor, leaning against the wall. Aline fell asleep after a couple of hours. Doris and her sisters never relaxed their vigil, though. Their father would not pull the trigger as long as they were there. That was what they wanted to believe. He never looked at them. Until his arm started shaking, then his chin, then his whole body. He dropped the gun, leaned back, and closed his eyes. Four hours had gone by. Doris picked up the gun and ran out to the garden with it clutched in her hands. She buried the Colt next to the playhouse and sat down with her back to one of its wooden walls. Her right hand lay sweating on the little heap of earth beneath which the gun lay. She was quite sure she was the one responsible for everything that had happened between her parents. Her stubbornness, her impatience, but most particularly *that*. The thing she had done which lay behind all her parents' desperate clawings. She cut herself for the first time that night. It wasn't hard. Her father was asleep in an alcoholic stupor when she went into his bathroom and opened her forearm with his razor. For a split second, before the blood welled up, she could see the open flesh, a white cleft leading into the unknown that was the inside of her. And as the blood dripped from her arm and spread out into a branch on the marble bathtub, she was suffused with a new tranquility. Her limbs went numb, and so did the guilt that had her like a thief, caught by the scruff of the neck.

the spring outside is reluctant to show its kind face, but she can still smell Aline's body between the sheets. Her fragrant perspiration. Rosemary, rose, lavender? She badly needs a slug of Wild Turkey. Then she will open Gabriela's letter. Her headache comes in waves, seeming to intensify with each surge. Gabriela is waiting in the house a rancher lent her in Jalapa, Mexico, the land she loves, and Doris promised to be there a week ago. But she can't set out. She can't because she doesn't want to. And Gabriela is groaning in her empty house, in her body emptied of Doris. A few days ago Doris telephoned her. She imagined her voice would calm her. But Gabriela is hard of hearing, and these conversations fragmented by distance just make her more desperate. Try as she might, Doris could not hide her feelings. *You have a broken voice I've never heard in you, beloved, a voice like an injured bird's,* Gabriela said. She tried to tell her a dream. She knows Gabriela likes it when she tells her dreams, because it lets her touch something of hers that would otherwise be out of reach. But the thing was that while she talked, while she told her the half-real, half-invented dream, Doris was suffocating. She was suffocating because she was picturing Gabriela in that agony that overwhelms her whenever she runs away. She flees unreflectingly, without thought for the consequences, because it is a compelling need, the need to get away from that hoarse voice which yearns and implores and demands all that she cannot and does not want to give. *I am rash, remember that, and easily angered. And CLUMSY, CLUMSY. I am a drop of water in the hollow of your hands. I will be whatever you wish me to be, I will live for you and for as long as my heart and you desire it, you, my Doris.*

she sits back up. She needs a bourbon. She walks barefoot to the living room and grasps the bottle, which is still open on the table from the night before. Her glass and Aline's are very close together, half-empty and opaque, completely lightless. A mimesis of what she is. Still standing, she takes a swig that burns her throat. Aline's skin is white and fragile. Their two bodies intertwined must make a fine picture, she muses, while the bourbon starts to take effect. She feels a sudden desire for her. From the fridge she takes the orange juice she prepared the day before, pours it into a glass, tops it up with Wild Turkey, and drains it. It's bitter. That last gulp has left her feeling a little tipsy. Just in the mood. Yes, she wouldn't mind if Aline walked through that door. She ought to eat something, but there's been nothing in the house for days. She hasn't been able to face the street and the grime. She has no money either, barely enough for the bottles of bourbon and the taxis. She shouldn't have mentioned that to Gabriela, because now, as well as the checks, she wants to send her someone called Délano, a Chilean writer or consul, she can't really remember, perhaps both, to take care of her. But she doesn't want pity. Not from Gabriela, or from Señor Délano, or from anyone. She just wants peace. Perhaps not even that. She wants to be Doris. The person who got lost in the heavy drowse of bourbon, in the hunger for eternity that makes her seek out the great. A few years ago she sat on Thomas Mann's terrace as he talked about the light of Los Angeles, where he lived with his wife and daughter. Now Gabriela sings her songs from her girlhood. A privilege she does not want to relinquish but at the same time resents, just as she resents having drained the rest of the bottle, having a dry mouth, and wanting another drink.

The phone rings. It's Aline, to tell her she will call for her at five to go to a reception at the residence of a widow, Mrs. Odler, a woman of great culture whose salons are frequented by the city's finest minds. Aline has a voice like dry grass, silky and faltering. Doris lights a cigarette while she listens to her. She remembers a time they went sailing with Mr. and Mrs. Knopp, Aline's parents, on one of her father's yachts. Mrs. Knopp was sweaty and obese, sheathed in a white- and blue-striped dress. Mr. Knopp was long and milky-colored. A man whose whole life seemed to be concentrated in his well-shaped mustache.

She could try writing while she waits for Aline to arrive. But not the letter she owes Gabriela. She wants to write something for that world that, as Gabriela put it, still fails to comprehend her talent. She is not such a fool as to be unaware that this was said to comfort her, to mask the infinite disparity between them. But it is also possible that Gabriela's words contain an ounce of reality, and for that ounce it is worth trying. This might be the time. She doesn't know, just as she doesn't know what the passing moments might contain until they have been and gone and can no longer be seized. This gives her the feeling that life is slipping stealthily away from her.

She sits down at the typewriter and strikes the letter A again and again. aaaaaaaaaaaaaaaaaaaaaaaaaaaaaaaa aaaaaaaaaaaaaaaaaaaaaaaaaaaaaaaaaaaaaaaaaaaaaaaa aaaaaaaaaaaaaaaaaaaaaaaaaaaaaaaaaaaaaaaaaaaaaaaa aaaaaaaaaaaaaaaaaaaaaaaaaaaaaaaaaaaaaaaaaaaaaaaa aaaaaaaaaaaaaaaaaaaaaaaaaaaaaaaaaaaaaaaaaaaaaaaa aaaaaaaaaaaaaaaaaaaaaaaaaaaaaaaaaaaaaaaaaaaaaaaa aaaaaaaaaaaaaaaaaaaaaaaaaaaaaaaaaaaaaaaaaaaaaaaa

aaaaaaaaaaaaaaaaaaaaaaaaaaaaaaaaaaaaaaaaaaaaaaaaaaaa
aaaaaaaaaaaaaaaaaaaaaaaaaaaa, imagining that another
letter will come, and then another. But nothing appears.

She needs to see Dr. M. He can surely give her
something to help her out of this lassitude. In one of
their sessions, he asked her to note her dreams. And
she, to provoke him, went back the next week after writing up an erotic dream that she exaggerated to the point
of obscenity. Dr. M read it unperturbed, as was to be
expected, and congratulated her on setting about her
task so diligently. Sometimes she feels like punching his
nose in, pulling him down from that untouchable place
he has made his own and kicking him to a pulp. *Take
care of yourself, take good care! Please! And be clean and
good!*

she lies on the bed and opens Gabriela's letter. *It
is as though everything were a poem I was writing, Doris,
a life I had made up for myself, because it is not going
on, it is past.* She shudders. She knows she needs Gabriela as much as Gabriela needs her. But the last time
she was in Jalapa, a month ago, she was in such a rush
to get away that she just got on a train one morning,
taking nothing with her but her desperation—went off
kicking the air, as Gabriela put it in one of her letters.

When you are gone, I can be suddenly intoxicated with bitterness, a kind of hellish purgative that hits me in the gut and leaves me in my death throes, only without blood or tears—without relief. The words leave her distraught. But also irritated. Why, since she claims to love her so much, is she unable to understand that she needs to become something other than an appendix to the Great Gabriela? *I see no good reason at all for your rough, ill-tempered, and almost brutal attitude that last day. I was nagging and foolish, stubbornly trying to stop you leaving. But in that kind of attitude we indigenous Latins see only affection and attachment, tiresome and silly perhaps, but just that. No more.* How could she explain to her? How could she explain to herself?

she stares at the paving stones of the sidewalk as she makes her way to the liquor store on 109th. It is a long and arduous voyage. Everything grates on her: her high-heeled shoes from last night, her dress, the dark glasses that threaten to drop off at every step, the voices, the glum faces overtaking her, cart wheels screeching as they ply Broadway. Everything is noisy and vulgar. And yet there she is, walking toward her one hope of salvation. She enters the liquor store with the refined, measured step that she inherited from her parents and that conceals her urgency. On no account must the kind-looking, white-haired shop assistant think she is desperate. It is all done calmly and unhurriedly, as though neither of them knew that her life depended on a drink just then. She puts the Wild Turkey in her purse and walks back the ten blocks to her hideout on 119th as fast as her hangover allows. She is not going to invite self-contempt by swallowing a swift slug on a New York street. *I know that if you do come, you will only leave again, and I will suffer far more than I already do from seeing that life with me wearies you and brings you no happiness. I would rather you didn't come than see in your eyes—and sense in your silences—that New York is in you the whole time.*

She ought to call Dr. M and tell him she hasn't slept in three days. Tell him anything. But she doesn't, because Dr. M, instead of coming for her as she would like, instead of shoving her up against a wall and fucking her, would talk to her in his neutral voice, the same old refrain. When she is with Gabriela somewhere on the globe, she writes him long letters that he answers laconically, usually mentioning Freud and his theory of penis envy. Why does she continue her treatment with him? Perhaps she is awaiting the opportunity to destroy him, or at least to undermine that irksome and rather suspect confidence he has in His Freudness and, especially, in Himself.

juliana

juliana turned thirteen on the morn-ing of May 4, 1946. She would rather have done something else, like eat an ice cream in Mr. Angelini's ice cream parlor, but Ma made her go with her to the student residence where she worked. And there she was, following her along the gloomy corridors, her mother walking briskly and swaying her hips the way bitches in heat did. Juliana hated Ma walking like that, because it brought to mind things she would rather forget. Arriving at each room, Ma would knock a couple of times, and if no one answered, take out the bundle of keys from her apron pocket and open it. Once she was inside, the sash windows had to be opened to let out the rank smell of sleep, the floor had to be wetted and cleaned with a rag mop, toilet chains had to be pulled, and traces of excrement cleaned up with a damp cloth. Rumpled sheets had to be removed as well, and wet towels picked up and thrown in a basket so that everything could be washed in the basement. For days, she and Ma had been unable to enter a room on the first floor. Number 102. Each time Ma knocked, a girl said in a hollow voice that everything was fine, and that she should go back the day after. Ma shrugged and muttered: "Huh, good, one less rat's nest to clean up." It was odd for there to be a girl in a men's residence, but Ma didn't want to get mixed up in trouble; she had enough of her own. They were on the fifth or sixth room when Juliana felt the soles of her feet itching. It was time to get away. After all, Ma never noticed. Her thoughts were elsewhere. Juliana liked playing on the first floor, under the stairs, where she had her surgery. There she imagined people from the neighborhood coming to her with their problems. Young men who had lost their girlfriends, old people with fungus on their feet like her grandmother, children whose tongues had come apart from sucking too many sweets. Sometimes even witches and angels came, and Juliana attended to them assiduously, because you never knew when you might need their favors. But something stopped her on the way to her cubbyhole this time. The door of room 102, the forbidden room, was ajar, and light from it spilled into the corridor. She pushed it open gently. A naked girl lay on the bed, with her arms hanging down on either side. It was not the first time Juliana had had a woman's buttocks before her eyes. Only these were whiter than any she had seen before. When she was standing next to her, Juliana realized she was the girl who lived on the floor above her own, in old Joanna's apartment. She had turned up with three suitcases a few months earlier. Sometimes she spied on her when she went in and out, with a faraway look as though she were not really there. She wore fashionable, soft-colored dresses, and everything about her was, how could she put it...magnificent. Old Joanna had told them that she was a student and her name was Elizabeth. But now she was lying in front of her, and her eyes were open. A dark mole at the corner of her mouth made it look as though she were smiling. A notebook lay open on the floor to one side of the bed, as though it had fallen from her hands. Juliana backed away, but the girl's expression did not change. It was then it occurred to her that she might be dead.

"Miss," she murmured. "Miss."

Be alive, she thought, be alive. And then she said it out loud: "Be alive, be alive."

But she knew that miracles were like lizards all dressed up for a party they'd never get to. She ran a fingertip down the girl's back, from her bony shoulder blade to where the buttocks began. Her body was warm and cold at the same time. Like the dead pigeon she had found a few days before, outside the doors of her building. She touched her again. This time she put the palm of her hand to her cheek. The warmth was going. Voices carried in through the window from the street.

If her grandmother were there, she thought, she would start crying over the girl's body. She would say the dead had to be wept over, whoever they were, they had to be wept over even if you didn't know them. Juliana went out into the corridor, ran up to the second floor, and then went down again.

"Ma!" she shouted.

She heard the echo of her own voice colliding with the closed bedroom doors. She had seen a dead woman, and now she didn't know what to do with what the sight had left her with. The open eyes, the feel of the skin, the idea of a death that was not a pigeon's, a cat's, or an ant's. A woman she felt sure had died of love, like movie stars.

margarita

nymphs keep going in and out of the gates of Barnard College. All gleaming like newly waxed floors. I try not to think, so that my senses are alert for anything that might happen in front of me. But my mind leaps from one thing to another, unable to settle. I think and think. I think about the rings left by coffee cups on the table of our apartment in Condell Street, when Jorge and I were newlyweds thirty years ago. I think about the vertigo of the empty days. I think that any night Jorge could disappear again. I think about the squirrel that turned up at the window of our apartment on 119th the first time

Jorge didn't sleep at home. Its tail was at least twice as long as its body, and it sprouted from its back like a giant pom-pom. It looked at me with its shining eyes and never stopped until I looked away myself. Then I began to cry. I spent the night at the window, waiting for Jorge. I could see the lights of the neighboring buildings suspended in the dark. Happy souls, appearing before me like the life I had lost. I thought that loneliness became real at exactly that point where everyone else walks on, drives away, takes a train, a plane, an ocean liner, and you are left parked there like an old truck with no tires. The squirrel came and went. Like my rage and my urge to throw myself out of that same window so that when Jorge got back from wherever he was I would be a lump of flesh and blood waiting for him on the sidewalk. At some point I called my daughters in Chile, but neither answered. It was just as well. A desperate mother is out of place in her daughters' flawlessly happy lives.

I googled my squirrel next morning. It was a tufted ground squirrel, a native of the tropical forests of Borneo, where it mingled with orangutans, pygmy elephants, and rhinoceroses. Which explained the look in its eyes. That squirrel knew the world better than I ever would. I called it Popup. It came back the next day, and the next.

"Popup, Popup, over here," until one day it stopped coming.

Expiring for love is beautiful but stupid

From that same window, I see heads and bodies moving along 119th each day. All in a rush, all on their way somewhere. Bodies I imagine meeting other bodies at night in the dark: office workers, students, professors, fugitives, salesmen, emigrants from the former Yugoslavia, provincials newly arrived from some village in North Dakota, broken men, women who can't sleep at night and go through the morning with drooping eyelids, people who are infatuated, defeated, or simply not there. Sometimes I am at my station early, after a sleepless night. Jorge finds me in the morning in my pajamas, elbows resting on the windowsill, head on hands, watching the street begin to stir. Then he kisses my forehead, sighs, and picks up his briefcase. When he leaves, the treetops six floors down shake in the wind and whisper secret messages. Then my treacherous soul goes back to the well-known places: the memory of an afternoon at the beach, the girls racing around, the sun high, and Jorge snoring beside me, his swollen red face covered with sand; anything, really, so as not to lose myself in a bottomless loneliness.

One morning, looking out of that window, I realized that if I didn't find a way of becoming embodied again, I would end up disappearing. Like Anne.

anne, the security guard of the building the university assigned us, on 119th, was the first person I met when we arrived at Columbia two years ago. We didn't exactly become friends, because Anne spoke little, but whenever she did speak it was to say something startling: "If I had to choose one person in this building to survive a terrorist attack, it'd be you." She spent her days sitting behind the desk looking at her cell phone and eating fried food out of a grease-stained paper cone. She was obese and wore a uniform. She carried a gun. When you entered the building after opening both doors with your swipe card, you had to go up to her desk and place it on a device that lit up green. Anne would raise her black eyes, look at you, and take another fried ball out of her cone. Her chiseled features were striking in that bulky face. Her lips were fine and intensely pink. She wore her hair very short, as if she had cropped it in a fit of rage. One day she had a small blue bird pinned to her uniform. When I went up to place my card on the strip, I realized it was an embalmed hummingbird. I turned away in horror. I could feel her mocking smile behind me. I turned back and asked nervously: "Why the bird?"

"So they'll know who I am," she replied.

"So who'll know, Anne?"

"All the people who'd be cut down if there were a terrorist attack."

"But not me."

"But not you."

It was the first time I had seen something approaching a smile on her face. Then she buried it in her phone, making it plain that the longest conversation we had had so far was over.

The hummingbird was always pinned to her chest from then on, defiant in misfortune, stiff, a black pupil pointing straight out at you like a camera from Anne's heart. She also started reading a little blue book with the title *Vanishing Point: How to Disappear in America without a Trace*. She never lifted her eyes from that book from then on. She stopped eating fried food from cones and looking at her phone.

One afternoon three weeks ago, I came across her at Broadway and 108th. It was the first time I had seen her away from the reception console. She was leaning on a wall, her eyes boring into the sidewalk and her arms hanging down like two rags. "Hi, Anne," I said, but she didn't hear. She was engrossed in something I couldn't see. She wore a yellow-flowered dress and the blue hummingbird pinned to her chest. She looked like a giant doll. I had the urge to take her by the hand and draw her back to this side, to her paper cones, her uniform, and her pistol, but I didn't have the nerve.

The next day there was another girl on reception. I asked if she knew anything about Anne. She replied, without looking at me, that Anne didn't work in the building anymore. I asked her again the next day, and the next, and then I asked the cleaning women, the guards, the other residents. Evasive replies, blank eyes, silences. As though I were asking about the fate of the world, the future paths of hurricanes, something unknowable.

A couple of days ago, a woman intercepted me at the door of the residence. Her sudden appearance startled me.

"I heard you were asking about Anne."

She had the same lilting accent. And she had the same nose straight out of a painting. She could have been her older sister, but everything that in Anne conveyed contempt, in this woman was shrewdness. She wore a close-fitting dress, and her face was made up a shade more than was appropriate on 119th Street at midday on a Wednesday.

"Were you a friend of Anne's?" she asked. Searching eyes, like Anne's in their expression, but intensely blue, bored into me.

"Yes," I lied.

"No one was friends with Anne."

"Well, I am. Where is she?"

"She disappeared."

"What do you mean?"

"Just that. She disappeared. There's no trace of her."

"I'm so sorry," I said. I thought of the gleam from the gun that Anne carried at her waist.

"Is there anything you can tell me about her?" she asked. "I'm her mother."

It's amazing how a piece of information can suddenly reveal what you've overlooked. I realized that she must be well over forty, that she was on the verge of tears, that she had a festering pimple on her right cheek, and that crumpled skin showed through her makeup. She was obviously exhausted, exhausted from coping with a daughter who wore an embalmed hummingbird pinned over her heart. Over hers, she had an embroidered label that read *Paradiso*. On the sidewalk opposite I perceived the mysterious power of the trees, the way their branches spread to meet their neighbors'. Was that what Anne was looking for when she disappeared? That fantastic embrace?

It's crucial to have an active fantasy life

"This is my cell," said the woman, taking a subway ticket receipt from her purse and jotting down her number. "In case you hear anything, anything at all."

"Of course," I answered, putting it in my billfold. "Is this the first time she's disappeared?"

"Yes."

"Did you notify the police?"

"She left a note. She asks me not to look for her. She says she'll be fine."

We were both silent, looking at the ground.

"Well, I must go. Thanks anyway," she said.

We said goodbye. She took a few steps and then turned.

"You weren't a friend of my daughter's, were you?"

"No," I confessed shamefacedly.

juliana

she shouted again: "Ma! Ma!" And what if Ma had left her there, on her own with the dead woman? She ran out into the street and across Broadway and kept going until she found a small park to hide in, between the blocks of concrete. She curled up behind a bush and buried her head between her legs. The leaves had thorny tips that pricked her. But she wasn't going to move. Not until the dead woman went out of her head. Then she heard a female voice. She peeped through the branches. It was an older woman, but not as old as her grandmother. She was walking around and around the one bench in the park and reading out loud. Her face was as hard as stone. She was speaking Spanish, but her accent was not the same as Ma's or her grandmother's. She didn't use the same words, either. Some boomed, others gleamed, others again seemed to slither as quickly as the snakes in her grandmother's stories. She liked her voice. It was calm and hoarse, very different from Ma's, which always flared up nervously and then crumpled like burnt paper.

"What are you doing there, girl? Get over here," the woman called when she saw her in her hideaway.

Her grandmother had forbidden her to talk to strangers. The living creatures of the earth had been unkind to her, just as they had to Ma.

"Come on, girl, don't be frightened," the woman urged.

Juliana went over to her with her eyes fixed on the weeds. She didn't dare look up at her, because despite her best efforts she had shed some stupid tears. Juliana wore pigtails then, and she tugged them, which was something she did when she was nervous. The woman told her she had seen a cat.

"Want to help me look for it?" she asked.

They looked for a while, but when they didn't find it the woman invited her to sit on the bench.

"Now perhaps you can tell me why you were hiding behind those bushes."

Juliana told her about the dead woman and her intuition that she had died of love. The woman took her rather clumsily by the shoulders and drew her toward her. Her body had the clean yet worn smell of the towels in the student residence.

"I have died several times," the woman told her. "And I'm sure you will too."

margarita

the warm wind that is blowing up must be bringing rain. I wouldn't mind getting wet, sitting here on the Jenny Holzer bench on my birthday. It would be something out of the ordinary, in its way. I wonder where Anne is, what she is running from, who she is trying to be. I remember the little blue book she was reading in her last weeks as receptionist in the building. *How to Disappear in America without a Trace.* Once she started reading it, she was so engrossed she never even said hello to me again.

Why didn't I realize before?

It's started raining. Not very hard, but enough for me to get wet in my dash to

Butler Library. Once in front of a computer, I start searching. I discover that the story of Anne's little book is far more complicated and interesting than might be imagined from its humdrum appearance. The edition Anne had was the one produced by Susanne Bürner, a German artist. On the first page, the author states that it is a revised and improved version of an anonymous text from a website called *The Skeptic Tank*, which in turn is a compilation of recommendations from hundreds of people who disappeared of their own volition in America. When I looked up *The Skeptic Tank*, I found the same text, with someone called Fredric L. Rice fervently asserting authorship and complaining that for sixteen years the material had been purloined, doctored, and sold by artists and writers as their own. He must include the German artist in this gang. Fredric L. Rice describes himself as an old hippie, backpacker, walker, and cyclist who has lived on the fringes of society for decades, with long spells outside it. Another edition of the same text, unaltered except for the cover, was published by Seth Price, a successful Israeli artist living in New York, with no acknowledgment of Fredric L. Rice. In the library I find the version Anne had.

Confusing yourself is a way to stay honest

The first premise of the little blue book is that if you run from someone who's abusing you, that person will go after you. It's the law of the abuser: they need their prey to validate their worth. For that reason, he suggests promptly destroying the pursuer's automobile. There is a long explanation of how to go about this. Briefly, it consists in pouring grains of rice into the radiator. With this vehicle chapter out of the way, the hard information begins. Leave behind your house, your car, your cell phone, your clothes, your books, your credit cards. Leave behind your loves, your friendships, your way of walking, eating, dressing, breathing, laughing, speaking; leave yourself behind. And go like that, stripped bare, but strong, because what awaits you out there is far crueler than you ever imagined. If you feel like bursting into tears, go ahead, cry now, before you leave, while no one's watching—wipe the snot on your shirtsleeve and bawl it all out, the way sad, miserable people do, because afterwards there will only be "out there," and "out there" you will have to be always on the alert, always watching a world that will try to break you. It all sounds so sane that I want to find a hiding place and burst into tears right now. The recommendations go on. If you have cash, hide it in different places in case one of your stashes is found. Never seek help from any institution or person who might be connected to the state. Look for your allies on the fringes: petty criminals, hippies on out-of-the-way farms, rockers, punks, skinheads, New Agers, bikers. Follow their customs, obey their laws, be obliging, quiet, and clean. Places like gay bars are good if you need to eat and spend a couple of nights somewhere safe. Use disposable wipes to erase any traces you may have left behind. Whenever you open a door, go to the bathroom, pick up a phone, leave waste, your skin is always flaking off, your hair is tirelessly regenerating. At the end of a year you are not the same person; everything you were, biologically speaking, has been left on the road. Keep your hair short whether you are a man or a woman, wear a hat, gloves, use toilet-seat protectors—"ass gaskets." Never lick a stamp or leave traces of semen, menstrual discharge, or blood. If the authorities are after you, they will use latest-generation chemicals that detect the tiniest amounts of blood cells, and from them obtain your DNA. If you are good at surviving in the wild, get away from cities, live in the woods, nourish yourself with plants, breathe fresh air, until the hue and cry is over. A month or two. If you find a better life there than the one you had, stay longer, but not so long that you get to be known to hunters and farmers as the crazy in the woods. Once the critical period is over, look for day labor, work hard, and get money together. Create ties of affection. Help others. Be who you always wanted to be. Start your new life.

Is that what Anne was looking for? The little blue book does not go much into the reasons why someone might decide to run. But it's not hard to imagine. Abuse, poverty, calumny, dishonor, disappointment, sickness, hunger, loneliness, violence, fear, overcrowding, bankruptcy, betrayal, mockery, rage, defeat, hope too, a yearning to be free and to appear somewhere else as a different person.

juliana

that afternoon in the park, the woman asked what grade she was in, and Juliana admitted she had left school. She had to cook, wash clothes, clean, clean, clean, and help her grandmother, who couldn't move now. There was so much "give me my pillbox, my cigarettes, my slippers, a scratch" that Juliana was sure she would ask for her soul one day, all of it, and throw it to the ever-ravenous alley cats. Her grandmother did not actually say this, but it was the feeling Juliana had, that by absorbing her so completely with her demands she would take her soul one day. Her buttocks and the mock leather of the sofa she lay on day and night had turned into the same material. Wrinkly and grubby. She hated her old breath and the sound of hinges as the door to her mother's room opened and closed to let strange men in and out. But of course, Juliana did not tell her any of this. Nor did she tell her that the girl she had seen dead in the students' residence lived on the floor above her own. Perhaps she or Ma would end up getting the blame, as usual. Better to keep quiet and wait. She did tell her that she wanted to get out of there when she grew up. Out of that neighborhood, that city, that life.

"I had to do the housework too when I was a girl. When I was nine, a teacher accused me of stealing exercise books from the school. All the children in the village where I lived turned against me. I was expelled from school. And so that I wouldn't be branded a thief for life, they put on my certificate that I was leaving the school because I was mentally retarded."

The woman told her that she had learned everything else on her own. By reading and watching. Especially reading. Before she left, she drew a pitcher and a walking stick in her notebook, tore out the page, and gave it to her. She also made her promise to go back to school.

margarita

after reading the blue book in the library, I take it out and go into the street with it in my purse. There is something dizzyingly attractive in the idea of disappearing. But that isn't my plan. Not today at least. It has stopped raining, and the puddles on the pavement reflect the gray sky. I cross 116th and walk more briskly toward The Hungarian Pastry Shop, where my friend Juliana works.

Protect me from what I want

It's my lucky day, Juliana is sitting at one of the outside tables smoking a cigarette. She looks more tired than usual. She is seventy-eight, and life has not been as generous to her as it should have been. She learned to be a pastry cook by watching the chef at a hotel on Fifty-Eighth. She worked there for thirty years, and has been making cakes at The Hungarian Pastry Shop for two. She dusts off the chair next to hers with a cloth and invites me to sit down. We have got into the habit of talking when she has a spare moment and I happen to be passing by. We don't arrange anything because Juliana has no cell phone, but this way, relying on luck, we've managed to be friends. On the café entrance wall is a poster that says "Expect a Miracle Today," and those are always our last words to each other: "Expect a miracle today, my friend."

She tells me she had a feeling I would show up. I don't let on it's my birthday. I don't want to have to tell her that Jorge forgot. Nor do I get around to telling her that it's been a weird morning, sitting on that bench covered with Jenny Holzer messages and then trying to track down the caretaker of my building who disappeared. She doesn't give me time, because I've no sooner sat down than she says she has something important to tell me. From a plastic bag she takes a pencil drawing in a sumptuous gilt frame. She tells me the drawing was given to her by a woman she met in a park when she was thirteen, just a couple of blocks away. The death of a girl who was renting a room in the building where she lived and the encounter with this unknown woman are the clearest and at the same time most enigmatic memories she has of her childhood. They have pursued her all these years, because she knows those two events changed the course of her life. The next year, against all her grandmother's and mother's objections, she went back to school. She hasn't stopped reading since. Not just newspapers, to keep abreast of what's going on in the world, but novels and a smidgen of philosophy, which is what has given her the understanding of human beings and her own life that she has now. She is sure that if she hadn't gone back to school, she would have remained in the black well of confusion that her mother and grandmother never left until the day they died. She asks me then if I can help her unearth the woman's identity. I answer that there's nothing I'd like better.

"I knew it," she says, pounding the table with her fist and flashing her gap-toothed smile.

The drawing is simple. A clay pitcher with a stick propped against it. The lines are firm but not at all artistic—it is more like an illustration for a schoolbook. I ask Juliana to tell me everything that happened that day, down to the most trivial details. She describes the woman and the brief but significant conversation they had.

I look again at the drawing and take a photo with my phone. It reminds me of those clay pitchers often found with red geraniums growing in them in a corner of the gardens of grand Chilean houses.

"Juliana, I'll do what I can, but it's not a lot to go on."

"I know, I know, but it's spring, Margarita."

"So?"

"Spring is the season of women."

"And who told you something so stupid and corny?"

"My grandmother. Although actually she never left the house in spring because she got hay fever."

We both laugh.

I'm about to go when Juliana gestures into the café, where our motto is, and says: "Perhaps today?"

"Perhaps today."

elizabeth

Dearest Kristina,

Would you believe me if I said I'd done it? Well, I have! Here I am, miles away from Father and Mother's clutches, their mansion, their servants, their rules. I never thought I'd do it either. It seemed impossible. I got out one night, caught a bus at Mastic station, loaded up my three suitcases, and left. Now I live in Harlem, in a room I rent from an old woman called Joanna. She's Dominican. She charges me twenty cents a night. The building is falling to bits, and you never know which of the

drunks who live here you'll meet on the stairs. The
drunk from the second floor, the fourth, or the fifth.
Old Joanna's apartment is grubby and run-down,
but still a haven in this dump. She has artificial
flowers and little animals made of glass. Also two
pistachio-colored parakeets that squawk all day.
The old lady is toothless and deaf and spends her
time talking to a photo of Burt Lancaster while a
gutted transistor splutters beside her. One after-
noon, she told me she had seen death. I asked her
what it looked like: "Thick and washed out like the
smoke from a steam engine." Next morning one of
the drunks was dead. She's an aunt of Renata's, a
Dominican girl Mother hired in Los Flamingos to
serve her while we were on vacation in Acapulco.
Luckily we swapped addresses. She saved my life.
Besides this place where I live, she helped me get
a part-time job as a chambermaid in a hotel near
Penn Station. The assistant of the assistant of the
staff manager is an uncle of hers too. Renata says
everyone wants a nice white girl like me around,
and that's why things haven't been as tough for me
as they were for her. She says it without rancor,
as far as I can tell from her letters. I'm paid thirty
cents a day, so I can barely afford to eat, and I'm
so thin that I'm acquiring a tragic appearance I

think quite suits me. But the most important thing,
my dearest friend, is that I enrolled as an auditor
at Barnard College. Schiller, Beckett, Eliot! Don't
fret if you don't know who I'm talking about. The
point is they're poets, real poets, and I fall asleep
reading their verses. Last night I went up to the
roof longing to see death like old Joanna. I didn't
see death, but I swear that the building lights shim-
mered in the dark and were brighter, more mysteri-
ous and more unreal than the stars.

P.S. Swear to me by all you hold dear that you
won't tell my parents a thing if they contact you.
Swear it. Tell no one about me, and burn this letter
once you've read it.

January 18, 1946

Dearest Kristina,
I have a fever that's laid me low in bed. And while
I try to bring it down with wet towels, old Joanna
won't let up. She talks and talks and talks, and
since she can't hear, there's no way to shut her up.
Today her daughter came to clean and leave her
food. I think she bathed her too. She had begun to
smell of dead cat. I start reading a page of Eliot

and my fingers stick to the paper, the fever makes me sweat so much. I sleep, but wake unrefreshed, and my innards growl. The parakeets in the living room squawk as if they were being murdered.

Perhaps this is all a mistake. Perhaps my destiny is to play tennis, read D. H. Lawrence, walk in the sterilized woods of his novels and watch Father and Mother move through the salons of power.

Please, Kristina, don't dream of telling them I'm sick. Or my sister Aline. She loves to go through life looking free and easy, but with me she always behaves as though she were from the secret police and I were a criminal. So now you know, say a word about me and I'll never write you again.

February 6, 1946

Dearest Kristina,
On Monday morning I was smoking and reading The Magic Mountain on a bench on the grounds of Barnard College when the assistant of the great George Tillinger sat down beside me. He was intrigued to see me reading German. I told him it was my grandmother's language, and that she had been the person I loved most in the world. I told him

all this, and Leonard Edelman sat gaping at me.
I'm sure it's my bones, which are more and more
prominent, more and more tragic. Leonard told me
that Thomas Mann would be coming to Columbia
in spring. He would let me know. Then he got up,
nodded, and left. I tried to go on reading, but the
birds cheeped wildly and the trees in the park strove
shamelessly to explode, breaking my concentration.

I ran into him again on Tuesday and Wednes-
day in the corridor. He stopped in front of me
both times as though he had something to say, but
just nodded and walked on. He walks like a baby
giraffe and looks out of place everywhere, which is
rather sweet. He finally spoke to me again today.
He told me President Truman was coming next
week to give a talk at the university and asked if
I'd like to go with him. How about that, Kristina?
I'm going to hear the President of the United
States! Leonard Edelman isn't handsome. At least
not the way we usually find men handsome. His
nose is bony and protruding and his clothes are too
small for him. He smokes the whole time, and the
lapels of his jacket are always covered with ash.
Besides, he's older, he must be nearly thirty. I think
he's even more desperate than me. But he's sweet,
he hardly dares look me in the eye, and unlike the

other boys he's not trying to get me up against a wall as soon as I drop my guard.

I miss you, Kristina. I haven't met anyone apart from old Joanna and Leonard. I'm scared of being found out and ending up back in Mastic. Leonard doesn't care about me being a fugitive from society, in fact he likes it.

I caught sight of one of the Dana sisters the other day. I think it was Doris, the childhood friend of my sister Aline. She was walking with Professor Neider, a Thomas Mann expert. She was talking emphatically, moving her hands, and the professor was listening with an indulgent smile. She looked so beautiful, so diaphanous, as though she had gone through a purifying filter and what we perceived of her was only her spirit. Even so, you can't know how scared I was. It was as if the whole of that life I am trying to escape had caught me again in its tentacles. But I also felt a tiny bit like approaching her, to feel the regard and warmth of a familiar soul. Sometimes, to be honest, I look at girls walking arm in arm without a care and wish I were one of them.

P.S. Are you burning my letters after reading them as I asked?

Dearest Kristina,

Leonard took me to a café at Broadway and 101st yesterday. Not one of those where the students usually go, but one where there were only old men. Several greeted Leonard. We sat at a window table and ordered coffee. Leonard opened a book and read me a poem of Auden's. The winter sun came through the window so strongly that it felt as if all the light in New York had been concentrated on our table. As Leonard read, his free hand crossed the halo of light that cut across the streets and the noise and the people and anything that might come between us.

Leonard is set on my being the best poet of my generation. He says I have talent but lack culture, and without culture poetry ends up tripping over itself and then failing. Although it may sound contradictory, he also tells me to write about my experience, that of a society girl who has decided to live with a deaf, toothless old lady. He insists I'm not to write about things I haven't experienced, because they come across as phony, like most of the poems by the people on my course. I disagree. Why should I only write about what I'm familiar with? Isn't writing a way of exploring? Besides, I

*explained, the place where what I write comes from
is below what I know and feel, in underground
tunnels where creatures with very stubby little legs
rush about looking for a way into my conscious-
ness, and when one of them succeeds I welcome it
eagerly, because I know it's bringing me something
I've never thought of. Leonard seized my hand
and kissed my fingers when I said that, as though I
myself were one of these messengers at his door. He
ordered another coffee, lit a cigarette, and told me
not to worry about meter, that all that was non-
sense and cramped the spirit. And him the assistant
of George Tillinger, the great metrical poet! I heard
him laugh for the first time. We laughed together.
I realized I liked being with him, I liked his laugh,
I liked everything around us, the sun, the smell of
coffee and the hopes for me in his adult eyes. And I
was afraid. Because what I have seen in my short,
limited life is that what makes you happy is what
makes you miserable too.*

February 19, 1946

*Dearest Kristina,
Yesterday we walked through Central Park, and
Leonard didn't speak to me the whole way. Nor*

when we sat by the lake. A few yards away a pair
of old men were bird-watching through binoculars.
One had long locks of white hair that grew out of
his head like weeds. The birds ducked into the lake
and then flew off, leaving trails of water and light.
Leonard watched them in a distant silence, hugging
his knees. "Tell me more about your mother," he said
without looking at me. Leonard likes me telling
him about Mother, he says she seems a remarkable
woman, and if he had Fitzgerald's flair he would
write a novel with her as the main character. I tell
him that Mother could only be a Poe character,
with her fits of rage, her morbid obesity, and the
fear we all had that one day Father would leave
her forever. But yesterday in the park, even though
it was he who asked, my words dropped into a
bottomless well. I did my best to bring us both out
into the light, but I sank into that well and sensed
that I could keep falling for the rest of my life. The
park had lost perspective and was like a backdrop.
Someone might topple it at any moment. I was
cold. But no, it wasn't cold. It was me. I struck his
chest: "What's the matter, Leonard?" I sounded
desperate. He took my hand and moved it away.
"Nothing, nothing's the matter," he answered with-
out looking at me. "It's not about you, it's about

me." Then he brusquely lit a cigarette, got up,
and set off along the gravel path. I followed. We
walked like that, he in front and me a few paces
behind, until we were out of the park. Is love a way
of being unhappy? I wondered as my heels rang
hollow against the sidewalk. On 119th we parted
like strangers.

I am frightened I won't see him again, Kris-
tina. And just the idea makes me more afraid than
I have ever been.

margarita

when we finish our coffee, I walk quickly back to the Butler Library, looking for some clue to identify the woman Juliana saw on May 4, 1946. I never imagined I would spend my birthday going in and out of a library. Outside the cathedral on Amsterdam is a woman lying against a wall. Her head and part of her torso are hidden inside a cardboard box, from which her dirty bare feet emerge. Passersby look at her unseeingly, perhaps embarrassed by the shamelessness of her predicament. The world finds nothing more obscene than misfortune on public display. Some newly polished men's shoes stand laceless beside the box. I wonder whose they are. I go up and give her a few dollars. "Thank you, may God be with you," she says in an educated English from inside her cubbyhole. And as I walk away, I think that maybe she's a scientist, a poet, a woman who took a misstep one day when there was nobody to lend a hand. Like Sylvia Plath when she turned on the gas and put her head in the oven, like Alejandra Pizarnik when she overdosed on barbiturates, like Alfonsina Storni when she walked into the Atlantic, like Anne Sexton when she turned on her car engine in her garage and sat waiting for death, like Antonieta Rivas Mercado when she shot herself with Vasconcelos' pistol at the altar of Notre Dame, like Virginia Woolf when she stepped into the River Ouse with her pockets full of stones, like Francesca Woodman when she jumped out of the window of a loft on Manhattan's Lower East Side, like the nameless girl who took cyanide in the bathroom of a mall in Santiago. Like Violeta Parra when she shot herself in the head.

I am awake in the place where women die

Before entering the library I get a Coca-Cola from a machine, and standing in front of the monumental portals of knowledge, dial my daughter Catalina's number. I know I shouldn't call, she spoke to me this morning to wish me happy birthday, but I do anyway. Whatever. She answers, sounding rushed. The turmoil must come through in my voice: "Are you all right, Mamá?"

"Yes, yes."

"Are you sure?"

"Why do you ask?"

"I don't know. You sound funny."

"You know I love you a lot, don't you?" I say in a rush of sentimentality.

"Mamá, something's the matter."

"I know, saying these things isn't my style, but I feel like it sometimes. Because time goes by..."

"It's true. I love you too, Mamá. Shall we talk this evening?"

"Sure," I reply, knowing we won't, she won't call, she'll be busy with the children, her husband, or some commitment of her Santiago life. I won't call her either. That's how it is. The seconds turn into minutes, time passes.

I down the last swig of Coca-Cola as intently as I will one day take leave of life. Perhaps to obviate the fact that I am about to disappear. I want to stop the first biped who walks nearby and ask if I look attractive, if I am actually a woman, a female, or just some creature with no race or gender that no one sees or hears, standing at some nameless way station. Instead, I calmly open my billfold and put away the coins the drinks machine has returned to me. That is when I find, forgotten, the subway receipt where Anne's mother noted her phone number. Her name is also on it: Lucy. I saw her daughter Anne several times a day for more than a year, but the image I have of her is vague, static, one-dimensional. Was it Anne who made herself invisible of her own volition, or was it us, the people who walked past her day after day and never saw her?

Do people disappear so someone will see them?

Impulsively, I dial her mother's number. She answers in a practical, neutral voice, like those telephone operators who take home-delivery orders. I explain who I am. I hear her light a cigarette.

"Have you heard anything about Anne?"

"Anne was reading a book, Lucy," I tell her.

"Reading a book, ah."

I can hear the disappointment in her voice. She must have hoped for something more substantial.

"A book called *How to Disappear in America without a Trace.* I have it with me. I think you should see it. Perhaps we can meet somewhere. I have time." Time is the only thing I have. "I could do it today."

We agree to meet at her place at half past six that evening. She gives me the address and we hang up. It's not far, at 146th and Broadway.

It can be startling to see someone's breath

I enter the library and sit in front of a computer. Juliana's encounter with the mystery woman was more than sixty years ago. I look for photographs of that time. It is a black-and-white world, somber and yet paradoxically glamorous. I marshal the meager information I have: a woman who read aloud in a park, smelled clean, and invented a lost cat to bring a girl out of herself. I try various paths that instinct suggests to me. All lead nowhere. A big man with hair in his ears sits down opposite me. I ignore him, he ignores me. Or perhaps I should put it the other way around: he ignores me, I ignore him. The time comes when I can't think where else to look. I study the drawing of the pitcher on my cell phone. So Chilean looking. And if the woman were from Chile? But what was a Chilean doing there talking to herself in 1946? Then I remember something crucial. The first thing Chileans learn when they set foot in Columbia is that it was here, at the Hispanic Institute, that Gabriela Mistral's *Desolation* was brought out for the first time. Before the poet was even published in Chile or any other Spanish-speaking country. I keep searching. And what I find exceeds all my expectations of what a bumbling investigator like myself might accomplish. I go outside. The sun after the rain strikes the white walls of the Butler Library and blinds me. A girl in flowery sneakers tugs someone who must be her boyfriend up the monumental steps while she takes selfies. I look for a place on the lawn under a tree and call The Hungarian Pastry Shop. A woman's voice thinned by the smoke of too many cigarettes answers. I ask for Juliana. A couple of seconds later she is at the phone. She is hard of hearing and I have to shout.

"Juliana, do you think the woman could have been Chilean like me?"

"Noooooo, never," she says. "You speak badly, and she spoke nicely, I told you. Is that why you're calling?"

"Are you sure?"

"Absolutely, Margarita."

"Listen. Three days after you met that woman, on May 7, a very important Chilean poet, Gabriela Mistral, gave a talk at Barnard College, half a block from the park."

"Three days later?"

"Yes."

"And what was she doing there three days before?"

"Practicing her speech."

"Three days to practice her speech?"

"Hm . . . you're right, it doesn't make much sense."

"It doesn't. And now I must go. I have some scones in the oven."

"Looks as if the miracle won't be happening today either," I say, not altogether defeated, but on my way there.

"The day's not over yet," she answers, and she hangs up.

I'm left with my phone in my hand watching the girl and her now-tame boyfriend at the top of the steps on their selfie crusade.

I still have time to make some inquiries before I meet up with Lucy. If Gabriela Mistral's talk was at Barnard College, then that school's library is where I need to look for the details. I cross Broadway, and a few minutes later am at a computer in the room where a temporary library has been installed, while the real one is refurbished. After a while I find several documents dealing with the event, although the text of the talk itself is not to be had. Documents like the program, the guest list, a number of letters sent back and forth to arrange the visit, insubstantial papers that are now part of the legacy left to the college by Gabriela's executor, Doris Dana. I find nothing that helps confirm the poet was in the vicinity of Barnard College three days before her talk, that she met a Dominican girl in a park, and that she changed her life. And yet, and yet... there is nothing to disprove it either. If Juliana had a cell phone I would send her a picture of Gabriela from those years right now. Perhaps she would recognize her. I look at the time. I can just make my appointment with Lucy. Tomorrow I'll be outside The Hungarian Pastry Shop when it opens with a photo of Gabriela Mistral, and perhaps the mystery will be cleared up. I leave the library and set off toward Broadway feeling quite pleased with myself.

elizabeth

Dearest Kristina,

On Monday we were strolling along Broadway, Leonard and I, and for the first time he recited a poem of his. It was about a farewell. I thought he had found the perfect way to get rid of me. I have always known that from a distance I have a kind of gleam, a brightness that turns out to be just a mirage once you know me. So I have known since the first day that it was only a matter of weeks, days, hours until Leonard realized. The time had come. My childishness and silliness

had been exposed. I couldn't speak. He didn't say
a word either. We kept walking nowhere, through
a no-man's-land that was frail, unsteady, and
sad. After a while, looking upset, he asked if I
hadn't liked his poem, if it wasn't good enough, if
I expected more of him. I said no, it wasn't that.
And he kissed me. Our first kiss. When our lips
separated, I thought that nothing that happened
in my life afterward would mean anything unless a
kiss from him was part of it. I realized that kisses
were like knowledge. Once they arrive, they stay
in you, and you want more. The mind and body do
not forget and are insatiable.

It's been several days since then. We have
kissed many more times now, whenever we can. It
is a kind of madness.

February 26, 1946

Dearest Kristina,
I enrolled as an auditor in a course on Pride and
Prejudice *with E. K. Brown, a well-known profes-*
sor. The novel starts like this: "It is a truth univer-
sally acknowledged, that a single man in possession
of a good fortune, must be in want of a wife." A
Mexican girl who always sits at the back of the

room asked: "Sir, can I say something?" Professor Brown, with his elephantine circumspection, barely nodded. Then she said: "In Spanish there's another issue here. 'Esposa' is the word for wife, but it also means handcuffs. The verb esposar means to fasten, immobilize, trap. If we think about it this way, we could give a more modern slant to Austen's text, for example that a man with a 'good fortune' can get a woman and cuff her to the foot of his bed for the rest of her life." Everyone laughed, even Professor Brown.

I have also signed up for a lecture that Elder Olson is coming to give next month. I am reading his work. He published his first book of poems, Thing of Sorrow, at twenty-four. In one of the poems he speaks of light as though it were rain. It is such a beautiful image that after reading it I had to leave my room and walk with my heart pounding, imagining Leonard appearing at some bend of the street, spring rain coming in from lower Manhattan like light, and us falling down for love on the sidewalk, intertwined. I twisted an ankle on the way back and walked the last four blocks with my shoes off, clinging to walls and fences. I must have looked like a drunk or a lunatic. But I didn't mind the scornful looks. I felt I was entering another

dimension. One where I was free. I could sprawl
on the sidewalk if I wanted and look at the stars,
the shadows in the windows and the eaves of the
roofs outlined on the emptiness, because whatever
I did would be part of the poetic intoxication Elder
Olson's poems had given me. When I arrived, old
Joanna was weeping silently beside the transistor
radio, looking at the picture of Burt Lancaster.
A Cole Porter song was playing. I don't think
she could hear it. My first thought on seeing her
slumped there like that was not that I should com-
fort her—how despicable the young are!—but that
it was my duty to live soon, live all I could, before
the sorrows inseparable from life closed in on me.

February 28, 1946

Dearest Kristina,
My fever's come back. Joanna's daughter who
works at a hospital brought me medicine. She says
I'll get better, but it would be best for me to go
home. The wall opposite is so near my window that
it blocks out any glimmer of light. I miss Leonard. I
invoke his presence every minute of the day the way
believers invoke a manifestation of God. I dreamt
that Mother threw herself out of a window just as

I was crossing the sidewalk and fell on me. I woke up sweating even more. I didn't know whether to laugh or cry. I cried a bit, but ended up laughing like a madwoman. Imagine the scene: me crushed beneath two hundred sixty pounds of Mother. You don't have to be a paid-up Freudian to understand the meaning of that dream.

March 2, 1946

Dearest Kristina,

I am on the mend, but not well enough to go back to classes. Yesterday afternoon, Joanna's daughter came with her boyfriend, a big black man whom the old lady could miraculously hear without difficulty. Leonard turned up a few minutes after they got here. I couldn't believe it. My incantations had got through. He'd bought me a silk handkerchief printed with flowers that must have cost him a fortune. I tied it around my neck, and he kissed me. Then we all helped Joanna up onto the roof terrace. I forgot to tell you that she has one leg twice as thick as the other. We drank beer while the sun went down between the rooftops and disappeared. Leonard and I were drinking together for the first time, and it felt good. Leonard draped

his jacket over my back and put an arm around
my shoulders. The air stood open before us like
those promises of Reverend Smith's that made us
laugh so much, do you remember? I don't think old
Joanna and her daughter liked Leonard. I'm sure
they think he's much too old for me. But I'm not
going to make their worries mine. I've got enough
on my plate with my parents' worries.

The three of them went down to Joanna's
apartment, and we stayed up on the terrace. The
moon was rising behind the buildings. I thought
of the millions of people in the world who must be
kissing and loving each other, like us, under the
carefree light of that very moon.

March 9, 1946

Dearest Kristina,
Leonard rented a small room in a student residence,
and we meet there every day in late afternoon. The
first day he filled it with fresh flowers to welcome
me. Among the flowers I found a poem of Eliot's he
had written out for me. Let us go then, you and I,
/ When the evening is spread out against the sky
/ Like a patient etherized upon a table; / Let us
go, through certain half-deserted streets, / The

muttering retreats / Of restless nights in one-
night cheap hotels / And sawdust restaurants
with oyster-shells. *I read it over several times, and
the words entered my heart and weighed it down.
I felt the loneliness of the lines, which was perhaps
Leonard's loneliness, his sadness at life's ugliness.
Then I hugged him and whispered the poem's
opening words into his ear, you and I, you and I,
five, ten times, then we fell on the bed and made
love. We lay there in each other's arms for a good
while, until the light disappeared from our window.
He went back to Brooklyn, where he lives, and I to
Joanna's house. But everything had changed.*

March 12, 1946

Dearest Kristina,

*Yesterday we spent our first night together. He
told me it would probably never happen again. He
sounded so upset when he said this that I didn't ask
why. It's odd, you know? For all the exaltation, sex
produces sadness. Perhaps because you are touching something that you know is ephemeral, that
you know will disappear as soon as your bodies
separate and you each retreat back into your own
carcass. While we were both smoking a cigarette,*

stretched out on the bed, he asked me to read him a
few pages from my diary. He knows I always have
it with me. The leather-bound notebook my sister
Aline gave me. "So you can get all that rubbish
out of your head," she explained with her usual
derisiveness, as though she had a need to sully
her good actions and make sure of a place in hell.
I read him a poem, and he listened to me more
attentively than anyone ever had before. I felt sad
to have reached the age of nineteen without anyone
having truly seen me, but I went on reading, until
he interrupted me at the word "glare." We stayed
talking about it for a good while. I had never
stopped to think what it really meant. Sometimes
words are like those places you go back to time and
again and end up not seeing. According to Leonard, looking, taking time, and thinking about the
meaning of things is all we have. If you could see
our bed! It's so small we have to get our arms and
legs in a tangle or climb over each other to get in,
though if I'm quite honest that doesn't bother me at
all. I know we promised to talk about sex when one
or the other of us was lucky enough to experience
it. But sex isn't something you can put in words. I
don't know, I think that if you try to explain it you
dissolve it into commonplaces, and although we've

been doing it since the beginning of time, I promise
you there's nothing commonplace about it. Then
Leonard opened the sash window that gives onto
the street, and the night air came in. A luminous
Camel sign was casting its yellow gleams onto the
sidewalk, a black Cadillac with fins was heading
downtown, and a man was dragging a duffel bag
across the street. Leonard and I were naked. Let
us go, through certain half-deserted streets, the
muttering retreats of restless nights . . . *Leonard*
howled, and I followed suit. We laughed till dawn,
the two of us howling like wolves at the window.

margarita

at 6:25 p.m. I am standing in front of the street number Lucy gave me. It is a building of reddish stone fronted by a tiny hair salon called Paradiso. I look through the window: brushes, combs, curlers, scissors, hairnets, hair creams, hair clips, dryers, curling tongs, jars and pots of all sizes, everything in perfect order, like an obsessive girl's dollhouse. I go in and a bell rings. Lucy has an apron tied around her waist and is sweeping the floor. When she sees me she drops the broom and holds out her hand.

"Thank you for coming."

Under a table, a ginger cat the size of a fox is pawing its nose with its eyes shut.

Several sweet aromas mingle, separate, and are left hanging in the air like streamers. Lucy isn't wearing the heavy makeup or tight-fitting dress she had on last time. Her appearance is more natural now, but just as striking.

"Margarita, isn't it?"

"Yes, Margarita. Like the cocktail."

Lucy smiles faintly.

"We could use one. Where are you from?"

"Chile."

"There's a Chilean living here."

"Oh, is there?"

"Come through." She takes off her apron, folds it in four, stows it in a drawer, and takes my arm.

"Mole, come here," she calls the cat-fox.

She opens a door in the end wall that is hidden behind an old Louis XV–style oval mirror. I stop for a moment and do a twirl. The mirror has the virtue of making you look at least twenty pounds slimmer. I feel immediately comforted. Lucy notices my delight.

"There are customers who come just to look at themselves in that mirror," she tells me.

We go through the door, and a long corridor opens out before us, lit by bare bulbs and leading far along to a clearing of natural light. Mole steps languidly and haughtily ahead of us. An old lady who must be at least a hundred appears at one of the doors leading off the corridor.

"Lucy, something's wrong with my television," she says piteously.

"Can you wait a second?" Lucy asks me.

Mole rubs his back against my legs while we wait, and I am surprised to find it is not unpleasant. Two boys walk in front of us without seeing us; a woman leaves a bag of rubbish in the corridor; a man in shorts opens his door while scratching his testicles, looks from side to side, and then closes it.

"Celeste's TV died," Lucy comes and announces a few minutes later.

Lucy stops in front of the door where I saw the man in shorts and rings the bell.

"Joselino, go to the corner deli and get a bottle of tequila and a pound of lemons," she instructs him in halting Spanish. She takes a few dollars from a pouch fastened to her belt and hands them over. "And then make us one of those, you know, get going then..."

The man takes the money without a word, and scratching his backside now, disappears behind the door.

"Joselino is the Chilean," she whispers to me. "He spends his days knitting. He makes socks and sweaters with wool his mother sends from Chile. But you know, he says he's a painter." She loops her forefinger next to her temple.

She takes my arm, and the cat-fox-mole meows. We walk the whole length of the corridor. We stop by the last door, and she invites me in. It is an apartment as tiny as her hairdresser's. A bed, an armchair, a small gas stove, two chairs, a table, a screen with a Japanese landscape, and Mole's gutted bed are all the furnishings. Even so, the place exudes a touching sense of welcome. Perhaps it is the window, on the far side of which a tree spreads branchloads of pale green leaves. And the woodland smell, which is almost real, unlike those packaged fragrances they sell in supermarkets. I wonder how she manages it.

She asks me to sit in the armchair and disappears through another door, concealed behind the Japanese screen. At 6:45 on the dot my cell phone goes. It's Jorge. I'm not sure I want to answer. It rings for a few seconds and then stops. It rings again. I answer in Spanish.

"Hola."

"Margarita?" he asks.

"Who else would it be? You called me, didn't you?"

"That's true."

I keep quiet.

"Are you there?"

"Of course I'm here." I'm starting to enjoy myself.

"It's just that you weren't at home, and now it's past six . . ."

"I have some things to see to." I feel a wild, violent exultation.

"Things?"

"Yes, things, Jorge, personal things."

"Ah."

A trace of compassion creeps into my euphoria and I add: "Don't worry. I left a chicken and pea stew in the fridge. There's rice from yesterday too. Don't wait for me."

"Are you sure? Is anything the matter? Are the girls all right?"

Savor kindness, because cruelty is always possible later

"Everything's fine, Jorge, don't worry. I'll get home as soon as I'm through here."

I don't say where "here" is, and I don't give him an opening to ask.

"Okay," he says.

doris

she washes and dries the glass, holds it up to the kitchen window to look at it, opens the bottle of bourbon, and pours a generous stream that she tops off with orange juice. Yes, today's the day. With the heat of Aline's body still on hers. She hasn't told Gabriela what she's attempting. She is afraid that if she puts her ideas into words for her, they will come apart, grow insubstantial, like everything that comes out of her ever-muddled, ardent head. Sometimes she feels like one of those men and women who douse themselves in kerosene, set themselves alight, and run about while their bodies are consumed by flames.

She is trying to write a play about two old women in New York. In the Frozen Monster, which is what Gabriela calls the city when she accuses it of coming between them.

She dreams of it being acted on Broadway or on *General Electric Theater*. A dream she indulges in when the bourbon allows. For now these are just ideas, emerging glimmers, beings who move across her awareness, appearing and then running off as though playing hide-and-seek, tempting her to go in search of a shred of their clothing, a furtive touch of their skin, anything, just so long as it stays with her and then grows, fills out with something more than air and longing. She sits at the dining table with her glass in front of her and begins to write.

"I shouldn't be here, waiting for something that will destroy the wretched life I lead if it happens and cast me back into uncertainty if it doesn't."

But who is this woman? Which of all the ones she has imagined? Perhaps it is herself. That is what Dr. M would say, and he would be right. Yes, it is she waiting for Gabriela Mistral, sitting on a bench in the grounds of Barnard College that May 7, 1946. She arrived early so that she could have a word with her before the rest of the audience crowded around the poet. She had put on a white blouse and a broad-hemmed black skirt, an outfit that gave her the neat, uncomplicated appearance she imagined would appeal to Gabriela. She imagined so many things. Her imagination had always been her advantage over the other girls, and her curse at the same time. She remembered Aschenbach—to her, Thomas Mann's most moving character—thrown into confusion by the sight of Tadzio racing through the waves on his slim legs, his fine pale face upturned, curls damp, and then Aschenbach's need to slake, with disgust, the rush of passion these images released in him. She had worshipped Mann for revealing to her the intricate paths that could be taken to deal with forbidden passions. They could always be gotten up in the innocent-seeming guise of some mystical feeling, which was what Aschenbach did. Gabriela Mistral's poems also possessed that hidden passion.

When she saw her go by that afternoon, already thronged by admirers, she leapt to her feet. She lifted her head, showing off a neck she knew was long and delicate, and stood there, observing the poet's distinctively awkward gait. It was then that she saw the agony in her eyes and lost the courage to approach her. Later she would learn that Yin Yin, her adoptive son, had killed himself and that Gabriela had lived in darkness ever since. She hung back from her entourage and sat several rows from the podium. Gabriela spoke of the industry of hate and of intellectual vice, and her words, enveloped in that rustic voice she would grow to love so much, unfurled before her senses in multiple, simultaneous forms, like a kaleidoscope. A brown drop fell from the ceiling; perhaps a broken pipe. It landed with a tiny plop on the back of her hand, the hand that was waiting nervily for life to get going, for Gabriela Mistral to raise her eyes from her text and see the young woman with the pale, passionate face—like Tadzio's—who had dressed for her. In the coarse-looking older woman was something purer and at the same time more complex than anything she had ever known. That was what she wanted to possess that afternoon.

margarita

lucy comes in with a jug and two glasses.

"Joselino was a barman before he took to knitting socks, and he makes the best margaritas in New York."

"And you got to his apartment through there?" I ask curiously, pointing to the screen behind which she disappeared and then reappeared.

"This is a maze, my dear, any door can lead anywhere," Lucy laughs. "You know, like in life. Why don't you come with me?"

We walk out to the corridor and toward a small, unkempt garden that has hung on amid the concrete buildings. It reminds me of a raft sunk at the bottom of the sea. We sit on some iron chairs whose cushions seem to have been feasted on by a community of mice. From on high, out of one of the hundreds of windows, comes the sound of an electric guitar being plucked. Someone sneezes three times, a blue-headed bird alights on a branch of the lone tree, the cat-fox-mole paws at something or other, and Jorge is cleaning his teeth in the bathroom while humming a song from a Tarantino movie. It's always the same one: *I'm a long time woman / And I'm serving my time / I've been locked away so long now / I've forgot my crime.* Jorge takes his shirt off and tosses it into the linen basket; he runs a finger over his gums in front of the mirror, *Hmm, hmm, hmm / doo, doo, doo,* he puts on an old T-shirt and sits in his armchair by the window to read, happy because he's picked up some compliment, even if it is off the floor: a mention in some paper, a girl's or a female colleague's glance lingering on him for more than a second, anything that feeds his voracious, tottering ego. The sky brightens and displays its best colors before closing down. Lucy and I take a sip of margarita and clink glasses.

"Do you have the book?" she asks suddenly, changing expression, as though the curtain had gone down at last and now, backstage, the real show could begin.

"Yes, yes..." I say, finding it in my purse. Lucy takes it and turns it this way and that to look at it as though it were some strange artifact.

"What does it say?" she asks.

I tell her roughly what I have read. About not leaving traces of hair, skin, or blood, about looking for work on farms, in Navajo tribes, and being nice to the people you meet on the road, about going into the woods and living outdoors. I skip the more unpalatable details, like the possibility of winding up in a ditch, frozen or decaying, and being found by a dog.

"My God," Lucy says, taking a long drink of her margarita. "I don't know, I don't know, I can't imagine Anne in any of those places you're talking about, and I can't imagine she's running from anything or anyone. She has no boyfriend that I know of. As a girl, she hated me. She hated the salon, the smell of shampoo, everything I did. But what she hated most about me was that I never told her who her father was. But not now, she doesn't care anymore..."

"Did she live here with you before she disappeared?"

"No, no. She lived in an apartment they gave her in the building, you know, where you live. In the basement. It had no windows, but it was clean and comfortable, she was all right there... alone, the way she likes

it, she could shower every day, she had a job, independence, and pretty much all that was required of her was
to be tough. Which is easily what she does best," she
says, sleeking Mole's back.

Mole wriggles out of her arms, and she leans over
to catch him. She shuts her eyes and tilts her head back.

Your oldest fears are the worst ones

Up above, in the patch of sky overhead, the last rays
of light break through a rift that is opening between the
clouds. In a tone of inevitability, monotonous yet firm,
Lucy starts to tell me.

doris

"*everyone i know*, every single person, is living now, at this exact moment, simultaneous with my own. They may be walking, writing, calculating, stepping around a puddle, eating fruit, lying on a bed looking at a crack in the ceiling, plunging into an icy river. Perhaps their knee suddenly hurts, or they've had a piece of bad news, perhaps they are thinking of me or have closed their eyes so as not to see something that hurts them. I've no way of knowing. But what I do know, what I am sure of, is that every one of those beings, whoever they are, is feeling and thinking," writes Doris.

She looks out of the window. The afternoon has settled. The sun is no longer sending out those rays that reveal the world's imperfections, that light that New Yorkers adore and that gives her a headache. She pulls the sheet out of the typewriter and reads over the paragraph she has written. More ramblings, as pointless as she is in person. She cannot concentrate enough to produce something that lives. She hears Gabriela's voice: *Look after yourself like something precious, because you are that, my heart. Foolish people have not known how to look at you and see you.* And does Gabriela know how to see her? Sometimes she is tempted to ask her: "Darling, can you tell me who I am, please?" She sees herself walking hand in hand with her two sisters through Central Park. She can't be older than six. It's chilly, the frost is spreading over the weeds and treetops. Her older sister is wearing a fur coat and looks like a miniature film star. A few steps back, her father is filming them. "Don't turn, just walk, that's it, holding hands like three little dolls, good, a bit more, I'm behind you ..." Then the hot chocolate and ginger biscuits at the Ritz, and the primped-up ladies squeezing their cheeks and flirting with their father, who hardly spares them a glance because he only has eyes for them, his little dolls. Of course, that was before she ran into his study one afternoon to tell him there was a dying bird in the playhouse, and found a pretty girl from high school with her dress over her hips and her father's hands on her buttocks.

She takes the sheet of paper in both hands, crumples it into a ball and throws it in the trash. Still two hours to go before Aline picks her up. She pours herself another glass of bourbon, stretches out on the bed, and closes her eyes. When the alcohol reaches her heart, time distends, broadens, and becomes like the endless season of childhood. That is where she would like to be. With her sisters. But the thoughts linger and release their poison in her head. Last night Aline told her she had met her stepmother at a lunch in Mastic. She didn't like her talking about that woman and her father. She feels that their happiness flows into her mother as pain, like two communicating vessels whose contents turn toxic as they move between them. She thinks how hard it is to make two happinesses coincide. Hers and Gabriela's, for example. She could try to answer her letters, but she knows that anything coming out of her pen just now will cause Gabriela pain. Just the thought of her is like a stab between the ribs. She loses strength. That feeling of falling into nothingness again. She covers herself with the eiderdown that still holds Aline's smell. What attracts her about Aline, besides her warm young flesh, is that, like her, she enjoys being both the femme and the butch. With Gabriela she only has one place, the one assigned her by her youth and veneration for poetic genius. A place that, forming part of the secret geography they share, is demarcated by the image of herself she constructed for her. "The dictionary girl," as Gabriela calls her because of her distant kinship with Noah Webster. For Gabriela, that girl can never be the butch.

she is roused by the insistent ringing of the bell. She looks at the wall clock. It is ten past five in the afternoon. She gets up, fastens her silk dressing gown, and looks at herself in the oval bedroom mirror. She raises a hand to her neck. Her white, plantlike skin is starting to shed its leaves. Time passes ... *I would like to go to sleep and wake up the day you arrive. Have we really lived through all this? Am I really going to see you again with these eyes of flesh and blood? Who do you live with? Your sister? What am I doing here?* The bell rings irritably on. A freckled errand boy has brought a bunch of white-and-yellow narcissuses with a card from Aline. They are the first of the year. She takes them carefully and puts them in a vase by the window. The narcissuses look almost wild in their simplicity. She stands gazing at them and for a moment feels good, as though the world were of her own making. She starts to laugh. It is a sour laugh, like the taste in her mouth.

*I KNOW, I KNOW that nothing could be more fool-
ish than to separate. People who separate may never meet
again, new interests may find their way into one of their
souls. In our case, that could happen to you, to you, NOT
TO ME, I assure you, Doris Dana.*

Time for a bath. Perhaps it will sweeten what little
soul she has left. When the water is coming out burning
hot, she holds her hand under the faucet. She wants pain.
She needs it. She thinks of Gabriela's sufferings. The sufferings that Gabriela bears and that she ignores. After
Yin Yin's suicide, Gabriela spent nine days in another
world. When she came back, she asked her friend Palma
Guillén: "Who was that woman screaming like a lunatic
last night?" "You," she replied. "That woman was you."

the doorbell again. It's Aline. She is car-
rying a bottle of champagne under her beaver-fur coat.
Doris, wrapped in a white towel, lets her in.

"I'm having a bath," she says. Aline tosses her coat
on the sofa and follows her.

"Did you like the narcissuses, DG?"

That was what they called each other as girls, DG
and AK, from their initials. It was the way men spoke
to each other. And now, when they are grown women, it
sounds just as provocative. Especially in Aline. Because

89

she doesn't smile when she talks. She never smiles. Even though everything she says has an ironic cast, a lazy, world-weary air. Aline sits on the edge of the bathtub. Her skin is sleek and healthy, the skin of a woman who has been massaged and pampered. She serves Doris a glass of champagne and lights her a cigarette at water level. Her straight-cut dark bangs and full lips painted in resplendent red heighten her air of defiance. Also, she smokes like a man. She holds the cigarette between thumb and forefinger, inhales intently, and then expels the smoke with an offhand violence. They toast. They toast each other through the steam that makes every-thing blurry and mysterious, they toast because Doris's father didn't pull the trigger that far-off afternoon in Mastic, they toast because their youth has not quite de-parted yet, because the world is a long way away, because their families didn't go under in the Great Depression, they toast because they are alive and want each other. They don't toast Elizabeth. Poor Elizabeth. Or Gabri-ela. Doris arches her back and her small breasts rise out of the water. *It's been a long time since I dreamt. So now I feel blind twice over—blind by day and blind by night.* Her pink nipples tauten and shine like two pearls. Aline brushes her right nipple with her fingertips, then leans over and passes her tongue softly over it until Doris feels it pulsing, like a small bird awakening her whole body.

margarita

LUCY: Anne was conceived by starlight on
the shore of Lake Henderson. What
an ugly word, "conceive," but there it
is, you understand. I'm sure it was that
night. The fact is I never knew what
they were running from. The pair of
them were too educated to be criminals. Roberto was Cuban, his was one
of those rich families that fled Fidel.
And Lancelot, ah, well, he really did
know it all. He had been to university,
an important one, I forget which.
ME: Lancelot?
LUCY: Yes, Lancelot. Roberto and Lancelot.
They were going from place to place

and camping outdoors, but they were surprisingly clean and well turned out. Looking at them, you might have thought they were electrical goods salesmen. Why did I hit it off with Roberto? I think it was because I liked life, you know, sunsets, palm trees, empty beaches, that kind of thing. But not to look at them on postcards, no, no ma'am, to go there and make love under the stars. That's what I imagined when I saw Roberto.

ME: Perhaps Anne went out looking for life as well.

LUCY: Ah, I don't know. I don't know what Anne wants. She's different. She's educated. She can do what she likes. All I had going for me was a good pair of tits. They'd have really come in useful if I'd wanted to be a whore, but that wasn't for me. So there I was. I was twenty and working at a cruddy hair salon on third.

ME: Your family's from Manhattan?

LUCY: No, from Bel-Nor, a town in Missouri with fifteen hundred residents. You can't imagine what it's like living in a town where your neighbor knows you down to the color of your panties. But Anne's not there. I've asked everyone. Anne hardly knows my family, I left when I was nineteen and never went back. My dad's a minister in the Presbyterian Church and my mom died.

ME: You were telling me about Roberto and Lancelot.

LUCY: Ah yes. Well, I used to go and watch the skaters
in Central Park every Sunday. I don't know, I love
that freedom they have. When they whiz by on
their skates and leap in the air. I watched them
from a way off, you know, because sometimes
they would grab any girl within reach and whisk
her away. I was doing that, eating a sandwich and
drinking a Coke, when Roberto and Lancelot
turned up. They sat down with me. They said they
were passing through on their way to Texas. They
were very, very nice, they laughed at their own
jokes. That same day, while we were drinking some
beers, Roberto invited me to go with them. Just
like that, "Coming with us?" And to be honest, Roberto was quite good-looking. But in a way, hmm,
how can I put it, like iron. There was nothing soft
about him, but at the same time everything rang
true, you follow? He spoke and moved like someone who knew how to get things done. And that
appealed to me. The guys from my town weren't
like that. Let alone the ones in New York. He told
me life without a home was hard, but that I would
have all the freedom I wanted. So, what can I say,
I liked the idea, and besides, I had nothing to lose.
The next day we met up in the parking lot where

they had left Lancelot's pickup truck and set off. We avoided the cities and spent most of our time outdoors, climbing mountains and sleeping in the woods. It was amazing. Manhattan had been the exception. They had stopped there because Roberto had had to sign some papers. They never told me what for. I never asked either. I never asked them a thing. It was enough for me that fate had put them in my path and saved me from living out my life in that crappy salon, where I was worked like an animal. When we got high, we'd go running into the woods, and sometimes we'd each go our own way; then we'd try to find each other by making animal noises, bears, wolves, birds. How silly. I don't know why I'm telling you this.

ME: What did you get high on?

LUCY: Oh, grass, hashish, nothing worse than that.

ME: Right.

LUCY: You know something? When Roberto saw me coming out from between the trees, he'd hug me and whisper to me that I was his Zhar-Ptitsa, which is a magic bird in Russian mythology that shines and shines, all the time, and is both a blessing and a curse for whoever catches it. That's what Roberto said, in those exact words. At the fireside one day they told me how they'd met. It really moved them to remember it. It was in the Virgin River Gorge in northwest Arizona. One night, when he was camping, Lancelot heard someone pounding a rock a long way off. He had walked a full day from the highway where his truck was parked and knew there was nothing for miles around, which meant it had to be another man like him, you know, a hermit. He went out looking for him in the morning. He found him on the riverbank, among the trees. Roberto had been there for three years, almost completely cut off from the world, imagine. All he had was a tent, a stove, a goat, and a motorbike. Ah, and a vegetable garden. They got friendly right away, and Lancelot moved his things over that night. They camped together for six months. Roberto had a daughter who knew where he was. She didn't like the life her father led at all, but she helped him anyway. They had a place to leave each other messages. A beer can under a rock, at the foot of a tree, five miles from his camping place, on the highway. It was a Carlsberg can, I remember that well because it was the only beer Roberto drank. He'd leave his daughter a list of things he needed, and a few days later she would take them to the same spot. Gasoline, books, tools. Sometimes, when Roberto went to fetch them, some hobo had stolen them and he had to ask for them all over again. That girl's patience, eh? One day, Lancelot suggested they go on the road together. A road to nowhere, as you can imagine. But that was how they got to Manhattan. And to me. You know? Sometimes I thank God for that, and sometimes I curse him. But how silly, I'm getting off the point, forgive me.

ME: No, no, please, go on.

LUCY: Want another margarita? We have to finish the jug.

ME: Sounds good.

LUCY: To begin with I only made love with Roberto, he was my man, so to speak. Lancelot often sat up outside, smoking his head off by the fire while we screwed in Roberto's tent till dawn. One night, Lancelot went in. That's how it was. Each one took me in his way, and they did it with each other too. The truth is I liked it. It was incredibly exciting. Oh God! I don't know why I'm telling you all this. It must be the margaritas.

ME: Don't worry about me, my lips are sealed.

LUCY: It's that it's been so long, and Anne disappeared...and I'm afraid for her.

ME: Please go on, all this might lead somewhere.

LUCY: Do you think so?

ME: I do, I don't know, but there's nothing to lose. Pour me another glass, please. These margaritas are terrific.

LUCY: Well, so we traveled for eight months. Think about it. Eight months! But one morning I woke up in Roberto's tent and I was alone. I went out and everything had gone. Roberto's bike, Lancelot's stuff, the stove, all of it. Just me and the tent. Alone in the middle of nowhere. I started screaming, "Fuck you, fuck you, fuck you," until I dropped from exhaustion. I went back into the tent, and next to my sleeping bag was an envelope containing five thousand dollars and a note from Roberto: "For you to start over, Zhar-Ptitsa." And that was what I did. I went back to Manhattan, found a place, this one, rented it, fixed it up, and started Paradiso.

ME: And did you ever suspect that could happen? That they might leave you, I mean?

LUCY: No, not at all. Although the truth is that we had been having problems toward the end. Lancelot and Roberto would argue over anything. Sometimes one of them would go off for a whole day and come back the next drunk or drugged. You know? They never knew I was pregnant with Anne. I sensed it the night it happened. You know these things. But I didn't want to say anything to them till I was sure.

ME: You never tried to find them?

LUCY: I thought about it, but apart from their names, Lancelot and Roberto, I knew nothing about them. They lived outside the system. They had spent years hiding, for all I knew their names were false. How was I going to find them? It was impossible.

ME: And did you ever talk to Anne about them?

LUCY: No. Not directly, anyway. I did tell her that I'd once had a couple of friends who lived outdoors, and that for years the only contact one of them had had with the world was his daughter. That really struck Anne. She always asked me to tell her about how they met in the Virgin River Gorge and how I ran into them in Central Park. Anne said these meetings were the result of something she called serendipity. I never understood what that word meant, but never mind. That's all. I never suggested to her that one of them could be her father. Never.

ME: And she knows you set off with them?

LUCY: Yes, I told her that I camped with them near Long Island for a few days, but it wasn't for me, too cold and dirty, you know.

ME: Hang on, hang on, where's the blue book?

LUCY: Here, why?

ME: There's something I need to see right now.

doris

"*Alg,* do you mind if we drop by a painter friend's studio for a few minutes? He's having a small reception to show his pictures to a gallery owner who's come from Los Angeles." Aline, cigarette in the corner of her mouth, rests a hand on Doris's shoulder and eases a shoe on.

"And that Mrs. Odler you sounded so enthusiastic about?"

"Mrs. Odler can wait," she says, running a hand through the air with a pout of indifference, perhaps to convey how New York *société* dotes on her and the liberties she can take as a result.

"Your mind's made up, then."

"It is."

Aline puts her arms around her, strokes her face, and smooths back her hair. The gesture is so exquisite that she knows herself incapable of resisting her whims.

"You're impossible," she says, and Aline lets out a guffaw. The first since they got back together the night before. She hasn't even seen her smile.

it's one room with peeling walls in a building on the banks of the Hudson, in the Village, where the artist seems to sleep, fornicate, and paint. A pair of sash windows provide glimpses of the sunset over the Hudson, a panoply of shapes and colors considerably more stirring than the triad of pictures of half-naked men and women against a maritime background that hang from the walls. Below, between the building and the river, is a garbage dump. The room smells of sour milk, sex, and turpentine. On an unmade bed in a corner, a boy and a girl sit propped against the wall, smoking. A group of young people stand talking in the middle of the room. Doris recognizes some. Scions, like her, of well-known families. There is a man with a woolen shawl draped in calculatedly casual fashion around his neck who just sits unspeaking on a bench, looking surly and smoking a pipe; he shouts out that he is "the artist." Aline leads

Doris by the hand and never lets go while she introduces her to the other guests, who look curiously at her, fete her and wait on her as though she were a celebrity. These attentions are pleasant. *I have truly searched my conscience and find only one thing to blame in myself: that I believed, from the flirtatiousness which is the way you treat almost everyone, that you had something akin to affection for me, and I acted accordingly. You should have given me a clear, immediate refusal. There was nothing like that.* Someone tells the story of a woman called Laura—everyone knows her—who followed a Portuguese sailor aboard a ship in New York Bay. Once out at sea, she discovered that the sailor she was so much in love with had a wife and child stowed away in the hold.

"It was the perfect moment for Laura to cast herself into the sea," says Aline. "Life gave her a unique opportunity to do something significant."

She draws on her cigarette and lifts her chin to expel the smoke. Everyone looks at the floor, unsettled by what she has said. She goes on: "I would have gone overboard off the coast of Amalfi. Wearing a bone-colored dress, of course."

"Laura's just fine with her family," says a girl who is toying nervously with her pearl necklace.

"What a pity..." concludes Aline, as if the whole story, with its insipid ending, were a waste of time. She half turns, and raises her eyes in search of a fresher and more rewarding audience.

Doris feels a sudden, deep malaise. There is a bottle of cognac on a paint-stained table. She reaches for a glass and helps herself. Nothing has changed here, in this universe she thought she had got out of for good. The same deviousness, the same playacting, the same eyes seeking other eyes' approval. *You don't know me well yet, my love. You don't know the depth of my connection to you. Give me time, give me time, to make you a little happy.* Gabriela's words form and unform in her memory. The thought comes to her that deeds and words usually go in opposite directions. Words are like winged insects that alight, weightless and unfixed, while facts creep along the ground, becoming soiled with earth and dust. She leans against the window. She wants to lose herself in that piece of sky where the frozen moon is coming up. She remembers those nights at Moss Lots when the house overflowed with lights and the servants hurried about attending to her parents' guests, all as young as they themselves are now. Doris would go out on the terrace and down the steps and walk along the highway that ran by the house, under a moon so cold it seemed to turn everything liquid. In these sorties she tried to take in what was too obvious to be seen during the day, like the cracked stones of the road, the way the trees' foliage came apart in the wind, and the air, which was simply there in the daytime, invisible, but became thick with damp at night and grazed her cheeks like a wild animal. Even then she knew she had to get out if she wanted to save herself. Did she? Save herself? She remembers a day when her father called them all together, the three sisters and their mother, in the room where he had tried to put a bullet through his head. He had seen to it that none of the servants were at home. It had been a long, wild day, the girls racing around the grounds, hungry, with no one to feed them, their mother shut away in her room in pajamas, and their father at the quay fixing one of his yachts, never lifting his head, too self-absorbed even to drive off the mosquitoes that took advantage of his inertness to devour his arms and neck mercilessly. When the sun went down he rang the bell, the one that proclaimed cheerful tidings. But this time its sound was hard and dry. And then they were all in the living room. Their mother was cloaked in a discontent not even the best-applied makeup could hide now. Their father was drunk—when had he managed to get into that state?—and crying. Pistol in hand, he threatened to kill them if they dared move. He didn't even yield when her younger sister, overcome by fear and exhaustion, began vomiting.

On the other side of the window, the dark waters gurgle along the bottom of the riverbed. White lights silhouette the boats as though they were under sail. It's well past time for the Los Angeles gallery owner to appear. The artist, wrapped in his shawl, smoke coming out of his pipe, shoves the young couple off the old bed and flings himself irritably down. Some young people sit beside him to comfort him. "You need to be patient, you know what gallery people are like," they tell him. Aline grasps her hand and they go off like that with a group of young people, leaving the studio and the resentful artist behind. They set off in two cars. The couple who were kissing on the bed climb into Aline's convertible. The woman is slight and dressed like a shop window dummy, with rose-shaped lips. The man, on the other hand, is tall, belligerent looking, abraded, with cheeks ruined by smallpox, and wears plumber's or bricklayer's overalls, although his very well-coiffured curls make it likely that he is the wayward son of some affluent family. They retract the roof and light cigarettes. Aline pulls away. Their laughter spills like thumbtacks onto the cobbled streets behind them. This might be what she adores most about New York, a life that belongs to no one and everyone, a life that pours into the street like sewage from a drain.

This being happy is a very rare thing, my girl. Happiness can be destroyed by tiredness—boredom—or just the passing of time. But I know that I have loved you from when I first saw you till now with the same enchantment as at the beginning and with a strange feeling that we have lived together for a long time, long ago.

After a few turns, they end up at Mrs. Odler's salon.

margarita

"what we need is another drink. Hold on, I'll be right back," says Lucy, disappearing with the empty jug through the door to the corridor.

When I look up, I realize that our square of sky has gone black, a solid, unbroken black, the black of gloss paper. I got five WhatsApps and four calls from Jorge while Lucy was talking. I cut him off all four times. I write him a message explaining I still haven't sorted out my business. "What business, Margo, what is it, can you please explain?" he comes straight back. I open the little blue book. What I am after is in the chapter called "South Western Deserts as a Place to Hide/Squatting," which starts on page 89. In this chapter, the author tells exactly the same story as Lucy did. One night, the supposed author of the book was camping beside the Virgin River Gorge, miles from any trace of human life, when he heard someone pounding metal against rock. He went looking for them in the morning. I get another message from Jorge. "Margo, it's your birthday today, I'm sorry, I'm so sorry, but there's been so much going on at the faculty." So much going on, I repeat to myself. The building walls reflect out the warmth. What's been going on?

When Lucy gets back with some cans of beer, I read her the passage from the blue book. She puts both hands to her mouth.

"My God! That's how Lancelot and Roberto met."

"How they told you they met."

"You think they lied to me?"

"I don't know. Anything's possible, Lucy. When I googled the book, I found someone called Fredric L. Rice claiming to have written it, but you see he doesn't even get a mention in this edition."

I get my cell phone out and google his name to show her. After presenting himself as an old ex-hippie, walker, and adventurer, he explains that he is now a respected engineer who repairs transport infrastructure up and down the United States. There's also a photo of him. He's sitting on a rock wearing a yellow helmet next to a couple of bulky shapes that could be a sleeping bag and a tent. He looks like the perfect American camper: direct gaze, wide jaw, and one of those smiles that confront life with confidence and an unnerving hint of beatitude. I show it to Lucy. She looks at it for a few seconds.

"Gosh, I don't know, it's been so many years. Maybe. He's got his look, his coloring. Yes, it could be Lancelot."

"Lucy, and what if that *L* between Fredric and Rice stood for Lancelot?"

"It's not impossible, no, ma'am." She opens a can of beer and passes it over.

"You told Anne about the meeting between Roberto and Lancelot, and she has to have read these pages. Like I said, Anne was engrossed in this book the week before she disappeared. Do you think the two things might be related?"

Lucy doesn't answer. We don't speak for a long time. Myriads of clouds have appeared in the black sky, moving surprisingly fast. It will probably clear soon. I hope so. I'd like to see some stars come out. "It's ten at night, are you OK, Margo? Please answer."

I take advantage of Lucy's silence to write: "Of course, sweetheart, everything's fine, relax." It's the first time in thirty years that Jorge hasn't known where I am. I hope this will soothe his anxiety. I haven't yet given up on my aspirations to be a kind person.

elizabeth

April 20, 1946

Dearest Kristina,

*I bought rice paper, black ink, and a
pen and spent the whole morning practicing calligraphy while the parakeets
squawked in their cage. It's amazing
what a peculiar quality the letters take
on when you draw them, as if they
were got up as something more than
themselves. When I was more or less
proficient, I copied out my poem with
the word "glare" in it. It's a love poem.
And in the afternoon, when Leonard
was asleep in our room, I slipped it into
his jacket pocket. I love that blue cloth*

jacket, the only one he has, with the pocket flaps
open because his hands are always going in and
out. Now as I write to you, my dear friend, I am
imagining how overjoyed he will be at finding my
poem in his pocket.

P.S. Last night I dreamt Leonard was screwing
my mother. You can't imagine what that was like.

May 2, 1946

Dearest Kristina,
I am writing to you from our room, where I'm wait-
ing for Leonard. I'm smoking a cigarette and read-
ing Virginia Woolf's diary. I shape a page or two;
and make myself stop. Indeed I am up against
some difficulties. Fame to begin with. *Orlando*
has done very well. Now I could go on writing
like that—the tug and suck are at me to do it.
People say this was so spontaneous, so natural.
And I would like to keep those qualities if I could
without losing the others. But those qualities were
largely the result of ignoring the others.

Time has passed since V. W. wrote Orlando.
She is no longer the same person, and whatever
was spontaneous in the writing of that novel is now

steeped in knowledge that she cannot and does not
wish to ignore, but that she fears could kill what
she had. I sometimes feel much the same. The more
I heed Leonard's suggestions, the more precise my
verses become, but they also lose what made them
mine. The night is starting to stretch out at the
window, and Leonard still doesn't come. I go on
reading, but the words go straight past me without
lingering. It's eight o'clock at night. It is impossible
that Leonard could have forgotten our appointment, as impossible as every light bulb in New York
shattering at once. Time passes. An hour, two.
There are moments when I think I've imagined
all this, Leonard, the room, Eliot's poem, just as I
have imagined Kristina. I can't even deceive myself
now. I would have liked to have someone like her
near to me. The patient friend who receives and
then burns my letters does not exist. It's just us.
The paper and me.

I undress and lie on the bed. I know that Leonard will appear at any moment and stop this drift.
Let us go then, you and I, / When the evening is
spread out against the sky. The woman who cleans
the rooms has knocked on the door several times. I
have told her, without opening it, that everything's
fine. I took some sleeping pills. I stole them from

*Mother before leaving. I'm not sure what I was
thinking then, perhaps I knew I would need them.
The way I need them now to wait for Leonard.
Through certain half-deserted streets, / The muttering retreats . . . Sleep takes me and carries me
off, then brings me back again. The colors fade. My
body, stiff with cold, folds up. Little by little, everything becomes unimportant, what has happened
and what will happen. Let us go then, you and I,
let us go then, you and I, you and I . . . I remember
the afternoon I saw one of the Dana sisters. She
looked so cheerful, so self-possessed. I imagine her
coming to save me.*

*The hours pass with exasperating slowness. I
go down into a dark place, like one of those spirals
I drew as a girl, more and more alien, more and
more unfathomable. Sleep alternates with waking,
the images are repeated, first one then another, a
carousel that spins in my head, until I am flying
through the air like a rag doll. And then it happens. The light bulbs of New York shatter and
throw out their expiring sparks.*

margarita

there's something I haven't told you," says Lucy.

She takes a few seconds to go on. I watch her expectantly.

"I bumped into Roberto a couple of years ago."

"Where?"

"Here, in Manhattan. I don't know if I mentioned that Roberto was older than us. I was twenty and Lancelot twenty-six, and Roberto was at least ten years older than him."

"I imagined, because of the daughter."

"It was a few days before Christmas 2014. I called in on Anne to invite her for coffee at our usual place."

Jorge is still sending me WhatsApps. "In the 1930s, when quantum mechanics was almost unknown, Schrödinger found something surprising that I want to tell you about, do you promise to read it?" "Yes," I reply briefly, while listening to Lucy.

"And he was there, sitting at a table, with his daughter and two teenaged grandchildren. I couldn't doubt it was him. The woman was at least twenty years older than Anne, but her resemblance to her was amazing. Even down to the obesity. She had the same matte skin, the black eyes, and that same 'I couldn't give a damn' attitude you'll have noticed."

"Schrödinger discovered that quantum particles that have been in contact can stay connected even when they are far apart."

"The two grandchildren," Lucy goes on, "were laughing and showing Roberto something on a screen, while his daughter was looking at her cell phone. Roberto was a mature man, you know, gray hair, blotchy skin, suit and tie, all very, very elegant. The opposite of the man I had known. Of course, I'd changed too, extra pounds, wrinkles, but we still recognized each other. He said hello to me and went over to our table."

"The fact that particles have interacted once means they keep their connection forever."

"We were nervous, you can't imagine how nervous. I don't think either of us wanted to remember, let alone for our daughters to know about our wild years. He asked me if I lived in Manhattan. He was passing through, visiting his family. I told him I had a hair salon in the neighborhood."

"Do you remember that Argentine physicist, Juan Maldacena? We met him once when he came to give a talk here at Columbia."

"I remember that Roberto smiled with satisfaction. He must have known it had been those five thousand dollars he and Lancelot left me that set me up in my own business. All his movements were very careful, he was like one of those rich guys in the movies, bankers, businessmen, you know. He held out his hand to Anne. "A very good afternoon to you, miss, my name is Roberto. And you are?" They looked straight at each other.

"Maldacena goes even further and proposes that two particles that have been in contact are not only connected, as Schrödinger suggested, but are always close. What he proposes, in essence, is a new conception of distance."

"I don't think I'd ever been so afraid, Margarita, never, ever. Roberto and Anne wouldn't take their eyes off each other. The whole thing lasted a couple of minutes. Roberto paid the bill and they left. He hadn't lost his way of walking, so manly. Yes, I know, I was still into him."

If anyone were to invent what is happening at this exact moment, it wouldn't be believable, and yet it's happening. Jorge is talking to me, but at the same time he is talking to Lucy about Roberto and Anne.

"That was when you knew, wasn't it?" I say.

"Yes. I had no doubt that Roberto was Anne's father. When they left, Anne bombarded me with questions. Who was that man, why had he and I gotten so nervous, why had he looked at her like that. 'Who is he, who is he?' she ended up almost screaming at me. I told her his name was Roberto and he was one of the friends I had met in Central Park. The characters in the two stories she had given that strange name to, like an insect's: serendipity."

"It couldn't be clearer, Lucy."

"What?"

"Anne went looking for Fredric Lancelot Rice to find her father. He's her only lead."

There's a contact link on Lancelot's page, a place in California called Cristal Lake Campground. I write to it. Lancelot is bound to answer. Now or tomorrow, but he'll answer. Of that I'm sure. Also that Anne is with him. I also sense that Lucy knew it, without realizing.

And what we've done is set things in motion together. Sometimes we just need someone to go into the cave with us so we don't have to face its truth alone.

"What I'm trying to tell you, Margo, like the clumsy jerk I am, is that I love you and I'm with you."

elizabeth

leonard comes into the room and sits on the edge of the bed. I hear his voice. What have you done, Elizabeth? His words are as hard as anthracite. I look at him, and a stranger's expression comes back.

He says his wife found the poem I wrote him on the rice paper. His wife? The poem that contained the word "glare" and spoke of love. *Let us go then, you and I...* She was ironing his only jacket so that he could look like the decent man she believes him to be, and she found it.

It's me, look at me, it's Elizabeth, your love, I just about manage to say. He talks on. Now his marriage—his marriage?—has come apart, his wife is crying and accusing him of adultery. His father-in-law has come to take her away. He has begged them to give him another chance. I try to decipher his words, understand what he's telling me, there is no logic in them. *Let us go then, you and I, / When the evening is spread out against the sky...*

Suddenly I know something for certain in my heart: it is not me Leonard has seen or loved, but the reflection of himself he found in my eyes. I don't have time to wonder if that is the nature of love, because a man with a top hat and a length of cord in his hands appears in the doorway. He is dressed with rumpled elegance, as if he has been out in all weather for a long time. I think I recognize him, but then his features become mixed with others' and he could be anyone. Anyone or no one. He has a small mark on his right cheek; it is a leopard's spot. *Let us go, through certain half-deserted streets...* I know from his intent look that he has come for me. He wants to shut me away. Other men have joined him, other men with hats and leopard spots who will carry me to a tomb. I scream. *Like a patient etherized upon a table...* I hear Leonard's voice. He carries on talking about his wife, his marriage, his father-in-law, while one of the men takes my hand and presses my fingers to the mark on his cheek. It burns like a candle flame. Then he ties me hand and foot. I see that Leonard is standing up. He looks at me and I look at him from the bed. What have you done? he asks me again, and leaves without closing the door properly. I raise the rest of Mother's bottle of pills to my mouth. *Let us go . . . restless nights . . . sawdust restaurants . . . one-night cheap hotels . . .* and I sleep.

doris

the widow interests her immediately.
Her eyes shine keenly, and her sharp face
contains the wisdom of those who don't
need much evidence to see people's true
nature. Despite her costly dress and the
glittering diamond brooch on her chest,
everything about her bespeaks a genuine
simplicity. She is sitting on a divan, and
whenever someone appears at the salon
doors she rises, half-stooping, to greet them
with a casual, absentminded air. Then she
goes back to her place, running her hands
over her dress as though it were a kitchen
apron, to continue her discussion with a pair
of older gentlemen by one of the lit fireplaces.

One of these old gentlemen has a red silk handkerchief tied in a flower shape in his boutonniere. They seem to be watched over by a large modernist portrait of a man whose elegance cannot conceal the grimness of his features. Perhaps it is the man from whom the widow acquired her current status. While Aline moves from one group to another greeting people, Doris goes up to them. The widow, without ceasing to pay attention to her companions, invites her to sit beside her and links arms with her by way of a welcome.

"The beauty of a mathematical operation lies in the cadence with which it discloses its truth, as in poetry," explains one of the elderly men, who looks rather like an old sea dog, tall and smooth-skinned, with a white mustache that wiggles while he talks.

"The idea, if you will allow me, is to make complexity transparent," adds the other old gentleman.

"Sorry," says the widow to Doris. "Mr. Cooper and Mr. Brenson are mathematicians."

"I see you've met," Aline interrupts with an unusually diffident air.

"Aline, darling, I didn't notice you come in," says the widow. "How good to see you."

"This is Doris Dana," Aline presents her.

"I know you're Doris Dana, and I am very happy to have you in my salon," says the widow, turning her level gaze on her. "I'm a great admirer of Gabriela Mistral. I gather you know her."

"Well, yes, I do…" Doris clears her throat.

"Some of her poems are heartrending."

"They are," says Doris.

The widow recites a couple of lines of Gabriela's. She declaims with grace and feeling. And for that very reason, because Gabriela's words come alive in Mrs. Odler's mouth, Doris feels an urgent need to have a drink, to make a small cut on the inside of her thigh or forearm. It has been years since she felt such a need to perpetrate those incisions that quieten her heart. Aline, perhaps aware of her distress, takes her hand. *The beings I loved never knew that I loved them dearly. But it is necessary for you to know. This I must have; I need you to know, to understand, and to want to live for me! For love or for charity, know it.*

"If you don't mind…" She helps her to her feet with a tug.

A huddle of younger people awaits them at the other end of the salon. Among them is the couple they brought in the convertible. Aline presents the others: Andrew, Mathew, Jessica, June, Leonore. They shake hands and then stand looking very seriously at the floor, as though waiting for someone to restart the machinery of social intercourse, but Aline, whose throat always holds an arsenal of superfluous words that nonetheless seem to spring from the profoundest ruminations, is already whispering into the ear of a young man with sideburns and a bandit's jawline, and Doris wonders yet again what on earth she is doing following Aline on her tireless journeyings. Then she sees him. It is Dr. M. He walks through the doors and toward Mrs. Odler with his sure, elastic step and that smug little smile she is sure he deploys to hide the monsters that assail him, as they do all other mortals. When Aline remarked to her that "the finest minds in New York" were to be found in Mrs. Odler's salons, she did not imagine that among them would be Dr. M, whose mind contains only the theory of the castration complex he assumes all women suffer from. She could approach him, but she wouldn't know what to say. She has never heard him utter a frivolous word, and she is sure that if one fell accidentally from his lips it would be swallowed up by his trim beard. It is the first time she has seen him outside his consulting room. At their sessions, she lies on the couch with her eyes closed, he sits behind her listening, and they barely look each other in the face. She slips away into a corner, pouring herself a helping of some concoction or other from a cut-glass bottle on the way. The widow stands up with her curved back and straightforward gestures to greet Dr. M. They seem to know each other well, for they chat animatedly. Suddenly she sees it all clearly. It is her opportunity to humiliate him. No, not that, just expose him as a human being. Aline is still talking to the boy with sideburns. She goes up to them and takes her by the arm. It is not hard to explain what she plans, it belongs to the sphere of action that Aline loves and where she feels most at home. She does not confess, though, that Dr. M is her analyst. She doesn't know where Aline draws the line and prefers not to chance it. She only asks her to seduce him. Just that. And to go as far as she can. As far as she wants to and can stomach. Aline walks haughtily up to the widow and Dr. M. In no time they are talking, and the widow is going back to the two old mathematicians. She watches Aline casually pick a piece of fluff off Dr. M's shoulder and whisper something in his ear. Dr. M laughs and takes her by the elbow, and they move together down the middle of the room. They don't make a bad couple. They both have a way of rising naturally above everyone. Each grabs a glass as they walk over to the tall windows that give onto the large balcony, where the lights of a chandelier overhead pick out Aline's splendid features. She never imagined it would be so easy. Dr. M is laughing and deploying an arsenal of gestures he has kept concealed from her. In short, he is doing everything a man eager to be chosen by a woman like Aline would do. It is almost ridiculously simple and commonplace. Dr. M reduced to the condition of a plain man. But now she'd like them to stop. She has seen enough. She fears what she might start feeling if they go on. *Last night I was able to REALIZE your face and I kissed you in it, morsel by morsel. How stupid he has been, my Doris, this one who loves you best! Forgive me, my heart, forgive me! I shall never do it again! And you will have control over your life, and keep faith with this poor old thing, who is clumsy, fervent and poisoned by his inferiority complex (that of age).* But at the same time, a part of her wants everything to be blown to pieces. Like when she saw her father's hands on the backside of the girl from school and started yelling so loudly that her mother and the maids were in the room just seconds after he'd fastened his pants and the girl had lowered her skirt. Those shouts triggered the collapse, and she could have quelled them if she had not given way to her need to destroy. Because she knew. Young though she was, she knew she had two choices: close the door and go on living in the quiet of a mirage, or shout it out and destroy it all.

she probably fell asleep for a few minutes. In the salon, a few couples dance to the strains of soft music from a gramophone. Among them she makes out

Aline and Dr. M. But she won't shout this time. She will withdraw in silence, take a taxi, and lose herself in the Frozen Monster.

You will find that I am a being who asks nothing of you. You will do as you please, you will have that absolute freedom you love so much, I shall ask nothing. I shall see you live and watch over your well-being. It will be enough for me to see you in this empty room, for us to listen together to the deafening birdsong (there are hundreds of birds on the grounds). I shall watch you live and that will be enough.

Your Gabriela

margarita

i say goodbye to Lucy and go out
into the street. I am a bit unsteady to begin
with. It must be the margaritas and the beer.
But as I move forward in the darkness, a
dazzling lucidity possesses me.

It is the first time I have walked through
this city late at night and not felt afraid. I am
not surprised. I have never been a coward.

A WhatsApp from Jorge arrives. "Margo,
Margarita, my life, please say something."
A yellow cab stops at the red light. It has a
Jamaican flag fluttering in the window. The
driver raises his hand and smiles at me, as if
that flag made him an illustrious citizen, a
friend to every passerby, the guardian of this

night and those to come. I smile and clutch my purse to my chest in a pointless mechanical gesture. I panic for a second, not because of the man now driving off downtown with his flag, but at the thought that I might have left the little blue book behind in Lucy's house. Standing in the middle of the sidewalk, I rummage in my purse until I have it in my hands. Now I know that its precious pages harbor hundreds of ways of disappearing. All praise to Jenny Holzer and that phrase of hers that I sat my ass down on today.

ACKNOWLEDGMENTS

To Melanie Jösch for her immediate and un-
quenchable enthusiasm. To Isabel Siklodi
for her close reading. To Ricardo Brodsky
for telling me about that first meeting between Gabriela Mistral and Doris Dana
at Barnard College. To Manena Wood for
generously showing me her documentary
Mujeres errantes. To the "Frozen Monster"
for showing me a piece of its soul. To Jenny
Holzer for inspiring me and allowing me to
quote her texts.

CARLA GUELFENBEIN is the author of six novels and several short stories, which have appeared in magazines and anthologies. Her work has been translated into fourteen languages and regularly tops bestseller lists in her native Chile. In 2015 her novel *In the Distance with You* won the prestigious Alfaguara Prize. Before becoming a writer, Guelfenbein studied biology at Essex University and graphic design at St. Martin's School of Art in London. She has also worked as an art director for BBDO and as a fashion editor at *Elle*.

NEIL DAVIDSON is a newspaper columnist, essayist, and translator. He has published collections of his columns as well as *El ceño radiante*, a biographical study of Gerard Manley Hopkins with new translations of his poems. Originally from the United Kingdom, Davidson now lives in Chile.